Swept Away By A Billionaire 3

TINA J

Previously...

IVY

"You scared me." I said to King who was sitting in the dark living room. After he taught me a lesson and promised it would never happen again, I fell asleep. When I woke up and saw he wasn't in the bed, I assumed he left.

"Come here." I made my way over and sat next to him.

"Ivy, let me start off by saying, you are the love of my life. I mean, you're the best woman I've ever been with, including my ex."

"Are you ok?"

"I'm going to ask you some questions and I expect the truth." Still not knowing what was going on, I agreed to answer them truthfully because I'm not hiding anything.

"What happened to you at my brothers BBQ?" Swallowing

1

hard, I told him the same story from before. He looked at me and shook his head.

"Did you have a miscarriage?" It was at this very moment; I knew, he knew the truth but who told him.

"King."

"How did you lose the baby?" I just started crying. What else was there to do? He found out and there was no reason to continue with the lie.

"Last question. How long has my aunt and Stephanie been terrorizing you?" No words came out because I was crying hysterically. He held his hands over his mouth like he was saying a prayer and that scared me.

"I protected you the best I could and the people you were scared of the most, the motherfuckers I should've gotten rid of been playing in my face this entire time."

"I didn't want you mad at them and... and... she raised you, and Stephanie was like your sister. King, I'm sorry."

"Sorry. You're sorry." He chuckled.

"YOU LOST MY FUCKING KID AND DISAPPEARED! YOU HAD ME STRESSED LIKE A MOTHERFUCKER TRYNA FIND YOU!" He was seething.

"I asked you what happened and you told me people fell on you. Ivy, they fractured your fucking ribs and you almost hemorrhaged to death." He hopped up off the couch.

"I fucked up by not telling you the truth about how we met. I even fucked up recently with my ex but I never lied to you."

"You didn't tell me about the ransom and how you planned on having me work in a basement."

"Exactly! I didn't tell you but you never knew so there was no lie told. When Stephanie shouted that shit out, I didn't deny it and what did you do." I put my head down.

"You left me again and of course I knew where you were but I gave you space. I deserved the silent treatment from you but to keep those secrets from me was fucked up." He left me sitting there.

"King, they were your family."

"And I told you plenty of times if either of them bothered you, I'd handle it. You never said a word. They could've fucking did you worse or even killed you and instead of saying something, you held it in."

"Excuse me for wanting to keep the peace."

"Keep the peace by letting them attack you. What the fuck is wrong with you?"

"King, you held out on how we met and—" He cut me off.

"We dealt with that Ivy so don't try an use it as an excuse." He opened the front door.

"Look, we've both done stupid things. Let's talk about this when we calm down." I wanted him to stay with me.

"I sung your praises to any and everyone who would listen. Shit, I thought Stasia was the perfect woman for me." I sucked my teeth.

"But when I saw you the first time, it was love at first sight and anyone who knows me will tell you I said that. There was something about you that told me, you were the one and Stasia was put out of my life for you." I felt like crap hearing him say those things.

"Yea my ex seduced me the first time and she kissed me earlier but what you don't know was, there was a gun to her head and I was about to pull the trigger right there." I was at a loss for words.

"That was until she showed me photos of her in Jamaica and someone spiking her drink."

"What?"

"It didn't make or break me but on the strength that she was my ex, I planned on looking into the situation as a piece of mind for me."

"Oh, so if she was you want her back."

"Not at all. I'm looking into it so if she didn't cheat and that did happen, yea it's fucked up but it only proved that she wasn't the one."

"I'm lost. How would that prove anything?"

"Because she should've never had a man or men in her room from the beginning and that would've never happened. If she invited them in, then it was what it was."

"King."

"Stasia was a grown woman and knew better just like all women who go away on vacation. There's danger lurking no matter where you go so allowing strangers in your room, she put herself at risk and honestly, the way she was letting them fuck her, it didn't look like rape." He walked outside and turned back around.

"Oh yea. When Stasia left, I sent Margie out there to give her a message and trust me, it wasn't what she wanted to hear."

"King, I'm sorry. Can you come back in? Please."

"Nah. I think it's time for me to do a disappearing act and see how you like it." I was getting angry.

"It's not childish or petty, it's called walking away from a situation before it gets violent." He got in his car and sped off.

I went inside, locked the door and headed to my room. Tears flooded my eyes and about an hour later, I dosed off only to be awaken by my smoke detectors.

Opening my eyes, I rushed out the bedroom only to see parts of the downstairs engulfed in flames.

"How the hell am I supposed to get out?" The fire was slowly creeping in the foyer so I had to hurry up if I planned to survive. I ran in my room, threw some slippers on, and grabbed my phone. Sadly, when I tried to hold on to the banister, my slipper came off making me miss a step and go tumbling down.

King

Leaving Ivy's house was hard because I didn't want to, yet I had to. I understand the fact she didn't want me arguing with my family but they could've killed her. Then to hear they were the reason she lost my kid made things worse for them. My aunt knew how bad I wanted kids and whether they were aware of her pregnancy or not, neither of them had any business touching her.

See, when Ivy disappeared the first time, that shit took a toll on me. When I found her and she gave me that lame ass story about people falling on top of her, I let her think I believed it. Little did she know, my ass was already investigating what really happened. I admit it wasn't easy finding out the truth but when you have a nigga dangling upside down with two gunshots in his body, he'll tell everything.

Liam, who was Ivy's ex had been sleeping with Stephanie for a while, even when he was dating Ivy. Of course she didn't know and it wasn't my place to tell because we didn't know one another at the time.

Anyway, my cousin must've been running her mouth about certain houses we kept drugs at so he decided to run up in one. One of the workers shot him twice, once in the leg and another in his hand, and this all happened last night. I always told them not to kill the person until we found out why they did certain shit.

Lo and behold, I had someone tend to the wound and waited for him to wake up. When he did and realized Amerius was standing there, he sung like a canary. Evidently, Stephanie was drunk and told him all the foul shit she did to Ivy. When my brother asked why he didn't say anything, he said because she was paying him to stay quiet.

The miscarriage and fractured ribs were a blow to my ego because I left Ivy in the backyard alone that day. I found out about that from Amerius who knew the doctor that helped her. I'm not even sure how it came up but I'm glad it did.

Amerius called when me and Ivy first got to her house, but I had plans for her ass and she damn sure didn't deny me. Ivy can talk all the shit she wanted but this dick had her stuck.

I really had faith in her to tell me the truth once I asked. Women always say, if someone asks a question you answered already, a second time, it's because they knew the truth.

For Ivy to sit there and lie in my face, hurt because the bitches in my family were tryna take her out and I didn't even know. They would've been taken care of a long time ago.

"Yo!" I answered the phone for Amerius.

"You there yet?" He asked about going to my aunt's house. He was supposed to meet me there.

"Almost. I'm five minutes away." Driving over there, Ivy weighed heavy on my mind. How could she not tell me about the miscarriage or them hurting her? Matter of fact how could she stay mad at me for that long when she had her own secrets?

Pulling into the driveway, Amerius parked behind me. We both stepped out and walked straight to the door. I checked for my gun, pushed the slightly ajar door opened and saw the house was fucked up.

"Oh shit. What happened here?" Slowly maneuvering through the house in case someone was still here, we checked every room and nothing.

"Is that blood?" He pointed to a spot on the ground in my aunt's bedroom.

"Damnnnnnn." Amerius said making me go to where he stood. My aunt was laid out with what appeared to be a bullet in her abdomen. Now the hatefulness I carried for what she did to Ivy, told me to let her dumb ass die right there. However, my conscience wouldn't allow me to. I called 911 and explained how we showed up to find her house broken in.

"Yoooo! Look at this." Amerius found a note next to the bed claiming that someone had Stephanie and they wanted fifty million dollars for her to be returned. All I could think of was Chris Tucker in Rush hour when the kidnappers asked for that amount.

"I guess her ass gonna die because I'm not paying that." The reason I'm here was to take her life myself for what she did to

Ivy. They saved me a bullet by taking her away. The ambulance showed up a few minutes later and took my Aunt Gloria to the hospital. Sad to say whatever happened here was most likely her own fault.

"What the fuck you doing here?" I saw Stasia at the front door peeking in.

"I'm here to whoop Stephanie's ass." She couldn't come inside because this was a crime scene. We were already here but they did ask us not to touch anything on the way out.

"Move." I pushed her out the door.

"King, she was the one who set me up in Jamaica."

"You just be talking. Go home."

"I'm serious. Look." She handed me some photos showing Stephanie in Jamaica standing outside Stasia's door with a grin on her face. There were also photos of her in the room watching Stasia and the other chicks have sex. I could ask how no one knew she was there, but if they were under the influence from the drug, I guess they wouldn't.

"How did anyone get these?"

"I don't know. Everything is crazy." Handing her the photos, one in particular caught my eye.

"Come here Amerius." He was standing by his car.

"Is that Darryl's arm?" Darryl had a unique tattoo on his forearm. It was a photo of the devil with an angel sucking his dick. I've never seen anything like it but hey, that's what he wanted. Anyway, in the photo you were able to see it but not his face.

"What would he be doing with Stephanie?"

"I don't know but she was the one who introduced me to Darryl. Oh shit." Amerius gave me a weird look.

"Nahhhh." I didn't have to say a word for him to guess what was on my mind.

"Think about it. She told me about Darryl and said he was a bodyguard. He was looking for work and told me to use him to protect Ivy. That's why he had photos of what they did to Ivy on his phone. He saw what they did and kept them. Fuck!" I shouted, handing Stasia the photos.

"Liam said she was doing foul shit to the women I dealt with. If Stephanie was in Jamaica, then she probably did set the entire thing up." I got in my car.

"King, what are we going to do?" Stasia stood next to my car looking stupid. That's as close as she needed to be. She won't put me in any more compromising positions. I know she came with those photos but she can't be trusted either.

"I don't give a fuck what you're about to do. I'm leaving." Speeding off, I headed home to figure this shit out.

"Yo!" I answered assuming it was Amerius.

"I suggest you check on that bitch, Ivy."

"Who the fuck is this?" The person had that voice scrambler on. I couldn't tell who it was or if it were a man or a woman.

"You're worried about me and that bitch probably already dead." The sinister laugh pissed me off.

"What?" I glanced at the dashboard and the person hung up. Making a U-Turn, I drove to Ivy's house. No matter how mad I was, it was my job to protect her. She'll have to stay with me for the time being. My house was big enough to stay away from her until I figured shit out.

"What the fuck?" I shouted in my car after seeing the flames. Ivy's house was still standing but the fire seemed to have engulfed the entire thing. I jumped out barely putting my car in park and ran over to one of the cops.

"Aye, did a woman come out of there?" The cop said he saw the firefighters bring out a person but they were put in a body bag. His words took my breath away. My knees felt like they were weak.

"Sir, are you ok?" I couldn't answer him. The phone rang again in my pocket and the number was unknown.

"That was a beautiful fire if I say so myself." I turned around to see if the person was standing there.

"We'll meet in due time but just wanted you know, I'm coming for you, but here's a gift." There was a pain in my right shoulder, followed by one in my side.

"Somebody's shooting." The scene was chaotic at this point. I was ok though. The shooter didn't get me bad. At least I didn't think so.

"We need to get you on a stretcher." A cop tried to walk me over to the EMT truck.

"I'm good." Seeing a shadow lurking between the trees, I took my gun out and pulled the trigger. Why the fuck was that person here?

"He has a gun!" The cop yelled. All I remember was getting placed in the ambulance with cuffs connecting me to the bed.

As the EMT's started working on me, the person came over with a smile.

"Hello, King."

"I'm going to kill you." I wasn't sugar coating shit.

"Not if I kill you first." I stared directly at the person when the gun went off.

Chapter One

IVY

SAME NIGHT...

"Dammit!" I yelled after falling down the stairs. My booty and tailbone hurt a little but I'm ok for the most part. Thankfully, I held on to the banister most of the way which kept me from flipping down the stairs.

"Oh, this is broken for sure." Still talking to myself, I stared down at my ankle; the same one that was sprained when someone kidnapped me.

Lifting my head, I saw the fire creeping into the foyer area. The smoke was now getting in my lungs and my eyes were starting to burn.

"I haven't found the bitch. Are you sure she's here?" I heard a man's voice. Not sure where he came from or how he was even in the house, I made my way to the door. Right before my hand could reach the doorknob, someone snatched me by the back of my hair.

"Never mind. Found her."

"Stop it. Please get off." The door busted open and firefighters were standing there with those masks on.

"Help me!" I yelled and felt my hair being let go. I'm not sure who the person was or why they let go but I'm happy the men were here. One of the other firefighters went past me. I could hear him asking where the guy went that was standing there.

"Are you ok?" Another man lifted me up to go outside.

"There was a man inside trying to kill me."

BAM! CRASH! I jumped hearing the loud noise.

"Well, if there was someone inside, he won't make it because one side of your house completed collapsed. The other half may do the same." Turning around, I stared in horror as my home was being destroyed. Who would do this and why?

"Here, put this on." One of the paramedics must've heard me coughing and rushed to put an oxygen mask on my face. The firefighter sat me on the back of the EMT truck.

"Do you have any other injuries besides your foot?" The woman wrapped it up in an ace bandage for the moment. I removed the mask to speak.

"The pain will come from this being my third miscarriage."

"You're pregnant?" I nodded and wiped the new tears falling down my face. I've come to the realization that I'm not supposed to be a mom. If I were, bad things wouldn't be happening to me. I can't even blame King or his association with bad folks because my first miscarriage was during the relationship with Liam. I still remember that.

"You're two months pregnant." The doctor said, walking in with papers in his hand.

"Really?" As bad as Liam treated me and the fact we broke up for the hundredth time, this was great news. I always wanted a kid; maybe not with him but hey, it happened.

"I want you to be on bed rest until you see a gynecologist?"

"Why? Is everything ok?"

"Your pressure was high and since this is the emergency room, I have to refer you to one. Also, this was your fifth time coming here for stress related headaches. Your weight dropped drastically from the last visit and that was three months ago." I put my head down in shame because he was correct. Liam had stressed me out constantly; sometimes so bad I'd get massive migraines; my pressure would be very high and I would stop eating. The relationship was taking a toll on me.

"Ok. I'll contact a gynecologist in the morning." He gave me discharge papers and a few doctors he knew that would be able to handle my situation as far as therapy. I started to get offended with him for saying I needed it, but the truth was, I did want someone to talk to so why not.

Long story short, I lost my baby two weeks later for the same reason. The stress was too much, the baby wasn't getting any nutrients from me since I didn't eat and sadly, my body didn't want me to have it. That was the only reason I came up with.

"Ma'am, are you ok?" I felt someone shaking me.

"What happened?" The EMT was staring down at me with a pad in her hand.

"You passed out after mentioning the pregnancy. We're at the hospital." As she spoke, the back door opened and two men were standing there. One was another EMT, and the other was a doctor.

"Her pressure was a little high, 149/96 and her breathing is stable. She also has a fever and she's pregnant." The female EMT gave them all the information on me.

"Ok. Let's get her inside; room five is open." As they took me in, the scene was chaotic. Nurses were running around; I saw some more doctors in another room and some of the patients were standing outside their room being nosy.

"Let's get her hooked up to a machine to check on the baby and order a dose of Tylenol." He let one of the rails down to do a quick exam.

"Contact an OBGYN and ask him or her to come down. Labor and delivery was crowded so she'll have to stay down here until there's a bed available." The doctor barked out orders and disappeared.

"Hey, you ok? What happened?" Rahasia ran in my room. Noah nor Knox were answering my calls and neither was Kandy. I hadn't spoken to them since yesterday when King picked me up from the hospital. She did text me that Noah was being discharged this morning and that they were going to his new house. She probably had her phone off and he was most likely asleep. I'm not sure where Knox was or why he didn't answer.

"I'm ok. Can you give me a ride home?" I stopped myself from talking and broke down crying.

"What's wrong? Are you in pain?"

"No, I just don't know where to go. My house was burned down, King basically left me and my brothers aren't answering." She walked over to hug me.

"Amerius said you're staying with us; well I told him you were." She pulled away and wiped my eyes.

"You can't be stressing my niece or nephew out." She rubbed my stomach.

After the doctor ran all the tests and kept me monitored for the last few hours, my baby was still alive and well. That alone made me happy, yet I had nowhere to go. My brand-new house was burned to the ground. I could stay with my father but did I really feel like dealing with ignorance.

"How can I stay stress free when my man left me, I have no home which meant all my mom's memorabilia was destroyed and—" She cut me off.

"And right now, you're ok. I know it's easier said than done but if you want this baby to survive, you can't worry about anything." I nodded and picked up my phone to leave. It was all I left the house with and it almost burned too if I didn't grab it up at the bottom of the steps.

"As far as your man, he's gonna be fine."

"You don't have to tell me. He left me and I'm sure went

back to his stalking ex. Do you know she spit in my face?" I told her walking out the hospital.

"Ivy, I'm going to tell you something but I need you to stay calm."

"If it's bad, I don't want to know." We walked to her car in silence. That alone told me it was and I didn't even bother to bring the subject back up.

"Do you want to stop by Walmart and grab a few things?"

"With what money?" I pouted getting in the car.

"Noah gave me money for you." I snapped my head in her direction.

"They're at the house. He knows what's going on and said if you didn't want to stay at my house, you can stay at his." She showed me the key.

I told her she could take me to Walmart and then I'd be staying at Noah's. I wholeheartedly appreciated the gesture from her and Amerius and would've stayed with them if there wasn't a choice. Since it was, I'd rather be comfortable at my brother's house. He just got new furniture too, I'm going to be fine.

Once we got to Walmart, I grabbed a few nightgowns, panties, bras, socks, some leggings, t-shirts and snacks. There wasn't anything else for me to get especially when this was Noah's money. I'm not even sure how I'll be able to get an ID without my birth certificate.

At this point, nothing mattered because I lost everything except my baby. When Rahasia dropped me off, I showered and went to bed. What else was there to do?

Chapter Two

KING

"Fuck! Where's Ivy?" My eyes shot open at the sound of a woman's voice.

"Sir, you have to relax. You have monitors on and you've been shot." Now that I was able to focus on the voice, I turned to see a nurse.

"Where's my girl?"

"She went downstairs to grab something to eat." I felt a sigh of relief knowing Ivy was ok but I'd be better once I saw her. It didn't matter what we went through beforehand. The only thing that mattered at this moment was her well-being.

"How long have I been here?" I asked as she fluffed the pillow behind me.

"Almost a day. They brought you out of surgery six hours ago."

TINA J

"Where did I get shot?" There was a bandage on my arm that was held up in a sling and I felt something on my stomach. I felt a little groggy but I'm alive and that's all that mattered right now.

"Let me contact the doctor because I just came on shift so I'm not sure." The nurse stepped out and in stepped this bitch.

"Babe, you're ok."

"Why the fuck are you here?" I snapped at Stasia. Before I was shot, she showed up at Ivy's house which let me know the bitch followed me.

"When you were in the ambulance, I ran over and you asked me to ride with you." What she was saying didn't make sense, yet how can I call her a liar when I didn't even know.

"You can go. I'm fine." She headed to the door and closed it.

"King, why are you treating me this way? You know the truth about Jamaica now. Why can't we be together like before?" Stasia removed her shirt and bra. I'm not gonna lie, even with being shot and this medicine in my system, she still had a way of turning me on.

"Put your shirt on."

"No one will come in because the door closed." She slid her hand inside her unbuttoned pants and started to play with herself standing next to me. This was not going to end well.

"Put your fucking clothes on." Trying to deescalate this situation wasn't working. Stasia pulled down the sheet to expose my lower half and since I only had a hospital gown on, she placed her hand on my dick.

"Stasia, you're bugging. Get out." Using what strength I did have; I pulled the sheet back up only to have her snatch it completely off.

"It's been a long time." She smirked and seconds later her mouth covered my entire dick.

"Get up." I used my hand to lift her head but the more I pulled, the more she sucked. The pain in my shoulder and abdomen was bad, yet there was no fight in me to stop her.

"Mmmmm. Cum for me like you used to King." The way she moaned while playing with herself and humming on my dick, I gave her exactly what she wanted. She got real nasty with it too.

"That had to be the best cum I've ever tasted." All I could do was close my eyes and hope no one walked in. I'm not gonna say it was rape because the nurses' button was next to me. I could've pressed it and didn't. What would it look like for me to call the nurse in and she slobbing me down?

"You gotta go." Pulling the covers back over me, she moved the chair closer to the bed, put her feet on it and masturbated.

"I miss you so much King. Yesssss baby, yesssss. I'm cumming." Her legs shook as she released.

The shit was sexy as hell and I had to look the other way. If not, I probably would've gotten aroused again. She may have given me head but there wasn't going to be any sex.

KNOCK! KNOCK!

"Hold on." Stasia was still sitting there trying to come down from her orgasm.

"Put your clothes on and open the door." Slowly getting

TINA J

dressed, Stasia told the person to enter and went in the bathroom.

"Mr. Miller, how are you doing?" A doctor walked closer and used the light in my eyes before doing an exam.

He explained that I was shot in the shoulder and abdomen which I knew. The pain intensified when Stasia sucked me off. He also said they were going to put a catheter in me, but my girl said she didn't want it and that she'd use the basin if I woke up to go. I was pissed because what hospital allowed that.

"When can I leave?" I needed to make sure Ivy was ok and it wasn't her in that body bag.

"I'm going to keep you for a few more days to make sure there's no infection." Stasia walked out the bathroom and spoke to the doctor. It was evident she lied to him about who she was in my life.

"Doc, let me be real clear before you go." He smiled and waited for me to speak. That same nurse walked in with a thermometer in her hand.

"This bitch is not my woman nor should she have been able to tell you not to give me a catheter; only a wife or husband can have that say and I'm not even sure that's possible." He tried to speak and I cut him off.

"I have a woman but because none of you checked, I ended up cheating on her since this one just sucked my dick and played with herself. Hence the reason the door was closed." His face was beet red and Stasia didn't have nothing to say.

"Why didn't you press the button?" The nurse asked.

"And say what, can one of you come in here because this bitch giving me head. Huh? What would you have done or said?" She shut right up.

"Now explain to me how I'm supposed to tell my woman, my future wife." Stasia rolled her eyes. I said that to hurt her for sure.

"How do I tell her the hospital allowed my ex to come give me head? Or that had you not knocked on the door she'd probably try again since I'm too weak to stop her. How do I even know if the bitch was jerking and sucking me off while I was asleep." I was pissed.

"I'm sorry, Sir. We didn't know. Let me get security." The doctor was very apologetic.

"What if she got sores in her mouth? Tha fuck!" The nurse had no words.

"King." Stasia tried to speak.

"You shut the fuck up. I told you to stop and even tried to pull you off but you took advantage and trust me, you will get what's coming to you."

"King stop playing. They think you're serious." Stasia was really trying to make pretend we were a couple.

"Bitch, I'm not playing. Get the fuck out like I been telling you for the last twenty minutes." The doctor and nurse turned to Stasia who appeared to be embarrassed.

"I'm just going to go. King, I'll be back when you get some more rest."

"By that time, Amerius should've been up here to bring my

gun and I will shoot you in the face." The nurse gasped and the doctor stood there with his head down.

"King."

"GET THE FUCK OUT! DAMN, HOW MANY TIMES I GOTTA SAY IT?"

"I think you should go." The nurse finally moved her out the room.

"I'm sorry, Sir. We're going to change your room and make sure that woman or no one else can enter unless they're on a list."

"Shouldn't that have been done for a gunshot victim anyway? And where was the cop that supposed to be posted outside the room?"

"I'm not sure what happened but we'll take care of it now. In the meantime, we're going to move you." The doctor said walking out.

"Why the fuck you still in here?" I barked at the nurse.

"You're bleeding, Sir. Your stitches may have busted open when—"

"When she was sucking my dick." I gave her a fake smile and told her to get the fuck out too and send me a different nurse. This entire fiasco was giving me a headache.

By the time another nurse came in, it was to move me on another floor. Once they got me comfortable, I used the hospital phone to call Amerius and he was already on his way here. I told him to wake me up when he arrived.

"Yooooo, she was giving you head." Amerius thought what Stasia did was the funniest shit ever. Ivy wasn't going to see any jokes in that whatsoever.

"Bro, I'm telling you, she did that to hurt Ivy."

"What you mean?"

"You and I both know she's gonna rub that in Ivy's face." I was being honest. The moment Stasia sees Ivy that'll be the fastest thing to leave her mouth.

"That means you better tell her first."

"Where is she?" Amerius told me, she was at her brother's house because she didn't feel comfortable staying at his place. I'm happy as hell she didn't lose the baby.

"The cops said someone was in a body bag. Who was it?"

"All they told me was when they kicked the door down, Ivy was on the ground saying someone tried to kill her. The person was in her house." He replayed everything the cops told him.

"What?" Why was someone in her house and how did they get in if it was in fire?

"Once the house collapsed, they went around the back and a body was lying there with his feet stuck under rubble." I shook my head.

"The person must've been tryna get out and got caught. The fire burned most of his body. I'm waiting for the man to be identified so I can handle his family and find out who sent him." I thanked Amerius for being on top of things when I couldn't.

"Who shot you?" He asked a question I didn't want to answer.

25

"Stephanie." I didn't know her voice over the phone because of the scrambler but once she stood outside the ambulance popping shit, I knew it was her.

"Hold the fuck up. Our cousin, slash sister shot you." I was shocked myself when I saw her holding the gun. I thought back to her standing in front of me.

"Hello, King." Stephanie had a smile on her face.

"I'm going to kill you." I reciprocated the same smile to her.

"Not if I kill you first." When her finger went to the trigger, I stared directly at her.

"You better make sure I die because everyone you know will be dead by morning." The trigger was pulled and someone pushed her out the way making her miss.

"Get off me. He needs to die!" I heard as the doors to the ambulance was closed.

"I thought she was kidnapped." Amerius broke me out my thoughts.

"She must've made that shit up to try and throw us off to get money."

"But why? She didn't want for nothing." Amerius was as confused as me on why our cousin decided to come for me. After everything we've done for them, being shot was my repayment.

"You think she tried to kill Aunt Gloria?"

"I don't give a fuck who she tried to kill at this point. Her soul belongs to me and if I find out she set Ivy's house on fire, you can be sure I'm gonna kill that other nigga she fucking with too." Amerius agreed that she had to go. There was no other option when it came to my cousin.

I wasn't playing no games with Stephanie. She should've killed me when she had the chance because I'm coming for her with vengeance.

Chapter Three

STEPHANIE

"I still can't believe you stopped me from killing King. Now he's going to search high and low for me." I told Gary, who was Darryl's brother.

It's been three days since I almost murdered my cousin and would have if Gary didn't stop me. Granted there were cops around but none was at the ambulance which gave me a perfect shot.

When someone screamed there was a gun, I had already hit King twice. Because I missed was the reason, I wanted to finish him off. I knew my cousin was about to go on a rampage to find me. If he didn't kill the love of my life, I may have spared him.

See, me and Darryl were fucking around for years which was how he got a job with King.

The two of us met at a bar and instead of going public with

the relationship, we kept it quiet. For years no one knew about us and why should they. People try to break you up with rumors and gossip. Neither of us wanted that and thought we did the right thing.

Both of us were messing with others to throw people off, hence the reason I started sleeping with stupid ass Liam. That man had some good dick but he was an idiot and sad to say, was still in love with Ivy. He knew King wasn't letting her go but you couldn't tell him shit.

Unfortunately, the night Ivy was kidnapped, Darryl was with me right before I went to my cousin's house. I decided to go see King because me and him hadn't really spoken since the BBQ.

Darryl was getting in the shower when I left and since Ivy was with my cousin, or so he thought, there wasn't a need to worry about having to keep tabs on her.

Lo and behold the same bitch, I went to discuss was there at the top of the stairs. Yes, King didn't know at first but I did and it's exactly why I let the cat out the bag. The uppity bitch needed to know her man was gonna kidnap her. She deserved to be ran through working in the warehouse like the other women. It's what she was chosen to do.

It wasn't that I hated Ivy because she was a loner and I didn't know her. I hated the fact my cousin fell in love with her so fast. We used to hang out a lot when him and Stasia broke up. King even made plans to put me on his team which was what I've always wanted.

I was supposed to attend that elite dinner in California with him to meet all the top dogs in the drug business. I was mad as hell when he told me, she took my place. I'm not sure what happened in Cali but he returned saying he didn't want me living that life. It was on from there and every chance I got; I'd terrorized the shit out of his precious Ivy.

My mother was a punk and didn't want to bother her anymore after the BBQ incident, but I didn't care. To be honest, she never had a problem with any of the women King brought home, it was always me. I would make up shit and my mother would believe it. In return she'd hate the women without knowing the truth.

Stasia was a bitch and sneaky as hell. I'd call her out on shit and she would run to King saying I had made stuff up and was lying on her. I was happy as hell when he found her stupid ass in Jamaica fucking and sucking those other men.

Anyway, Ivy ruined the relationship between me and my cousin and had to face the repercussions. I was going to do everything possible to make her leave King.

The bitch ran out the house mad that day and ended up getting kidnapped. Her family automatically assumed it was King's fault but I knew better. Shit, the second she did leave, I called Gary and told him to get her.

Darryl told me, he wouldn't be at the house when I came back because he had to follow her. Therefore, I did what needed to be done when it came to getting that billion-dollar money. Sadly, Darryl lost his life anyway for not being a better protector for that bitch.

Gary had no problem going along with the plan until he

found out Ivy wasn't in on it. So, I lied to him about the ransom but who knew he would let her go.

Long story short, Gary told his stupid ass girlfriend, who in return told King. Talking about she was scared and didn't want him coming after her or her family. I told him to kill her but he refused and said it was what it was. Now Gary has been hiding out with me at my house ever since.

"That's your fault. I told you if the plan was to take him out, start with the girl."

"Ugh, I did. The house was set on fire but your stupid ass cousin didn't get her out the house before the firefighters got there. Then, he had the nerve to die because he ran the wrong way." I was aggravated about his cousin not dragging Ivy out. The plan was to hold her for ransom again with King and her father. Why not get money from both?

"Now what?" I sat in the hotel room rubbing my temples tryna come up with another way. I couldn't return home or even to my mother's house to find out anything; especially when I killed her. It was an accident but then again, it wasn't.

"Stephanie what are you doing here?" She scared me walking in the living room. It was late and I thought she was asleep. Not paying her any mind, I walked on her back porch for privacy.

"Hurry up. We don't have all night to kidnap Ivy and hold her." Gary wasn't too keen on holding the bitch due to knowing the type of person King was.

"I'm waiting for King to pay."

"Wait! I thought her father was the one paying her ransom. After the first kidnapping went south, we made another attempt.

"I sent a message to him too."

"This shit don't sound right. That nigga gonna lose his mind when he find out she was taken for a second time." He was concerned, but in my eyes, he had no reason to be. King had no idea who was behind taking Ivy.

"No. We got this. Make sure you're at the house when he drags her out." He said ok and disconnected the phone. Unfortunately, his cousin died in the fire and the firefighters took that spoiled bitch out.

"Stephanie what have you done?" My mother was standing there shaking her head in disappointment. When did she come out here?

"Stay out of it." I walked back inside with her on my heels.

"Honey, it's time to leave King's women alone. We have money and—"

"And I want more. Stasia didn't even have King hooked the way this Ivy bitch does. Either she goes or someone paying money for her." What really pushed me over the edge was King crushing my windpipe. My hatred for Ivy grew and there was no turning back now.

"This obsession with Ivy is going to get me and you killed."

"How? King has no idea who took her." I shrugged plopping down on the couch.

"You're my daughter and I'm worried about you."

"Don't." I was my own person and knew exactly what I was doing.

"Let's call King and see if he'll forgive you." She walked upstairs to her room.

"Put the phone down." She turned around shocked; she had no idea I followed her.

"Stephanie, we have to do what's right." I heard the phone ring on speaker, pulled the gun out and shot her in the stomach. She dropped to her knees and held on the bed tight.

"You won't be warning King about anything." Her tears and cries didn't faze me one bit. Gloria was my mother and I loved her dearly but no one was getting in my way. I picked the phone up and saw she wasn't calling King, but 911. I used the butt of the gun on her head and watched her fall.

I tore her house up to make it look like a burglary and raced to Ivy's house. I couldn't take the chance of her getting away because Gary and his cousin messed up. If she was in the ambulance then I was snatching her out.

"Stephanie, we gotta get outta here and you keep daydreaming." Gary was in a panic for some reason. He turned my cell phone to me and there was a message from my cousin.

King: *You should've killed me when you had the chance. And just know that no matter where you go, I'm gonna find you.* I threw the cell on the floor.

"I'm out." Gary grabbed his duffle bag and keys.

"Really? You're leaving me after all we did."

"I told you not to fuck with his girl and you didn't listen. Yes, I helped but now that he knows who did it, he about to kill all of us and I don't wanna die." Was he serious right now?

"He doesn't know where we are."

"Not right now but I'm sure he traced your phone." It was at that very moment I knew we had to leave.

POW! POW! Bullets started coming through the hotel room door.

"Shit! I told you. Let's go." We ran into the adjourning room and closed the door.

When we checked in under my mom's name, something told me to get an extra room. I'm not even sure why but I'm glad I did. When we got inside, I threw the blonde wig on and rushed to put on the bifocal glasses. We had disguises for reasons like this. Once we heard the people in the other hotel room, we snuck out the door. Thankfully, no one was in the hallway. We raced down the stairs and out the employee entrance by the front.

"Hurry up!" Gary yelled, jumping in the black truck. As he sped, off all I could think of was getting King back. I'm going to get what's mine even if I die trying.

Chapter Four

KNOX

"Yes, Baby. Don't stop." Yasmina moaned as I hit it from the back. I had no business sleeping with this chick but certain things had to be done to clear my name.

One night at the bar, she came over to where I sat talking shit about how we weren't good people for beating her man up. She went on to say how attracted she was to me from the first day we met at my father's house.

Crazy as it sounds, I let her continue talking and learned a lot about her man faking which I knew from the day I went there. I also found out her man was cheating but she didn't know with who. Her plans were to sue me and leave him high and dry. Little did she know, I had plans for her as well.

"Who dick is better?" Yanking her head back to look at me, her eyes were closed.

"I can't hear you."

"Yours Knox. I don't want no one else. Fuck!" She released and her body went weak.

"Nah, you not done." I pulled out, removed the condom and waited for her to finish me off by sucking my dick. I never came inside her even with the condom on.

"Hell yea. Just like that." After she swallowed, there was a knock at her door.

"Shit. I forgot she was coming over." Not caring who it was, I went to clean myself off. Her apartment was decent for the most part but her bathroom was outside the room.

"Who you got over here?" The voice wasn't familiar when she opened the door.

"None of your business." I heard Yasmina telling the person to leave.

"It must not be your man because I'd be allowed in."

"Bye." I came out just as Yasmina closed the front door. She followed me back in the room and plopped on the bed.

"When you coming back over?" I put my clothes on and picked up my things to leave. I've never stayed the night and to be honest, the pussy was only mediocre. My pops didn't lie when he said it was just ok.

"I'll call you." Hitting her with the peace sign, I left quickly only to be stopped by her stupid friend who was outside at the club when I beat up Yasmina boyfriend. The same one who sued my father from the start.

"Wow! I see Yasmina cheated on her nigga for a billionaire." I stared at the chick for a moment. I'm pretty sure she's about to ask questions.

"All I wanna know is how do I get an appointment?" I stopped walking.

"Appointment?"

"I highly doubt you'll be making her your main so she must call when she wants some." Making my way to where the woman stood, she smirked when I got close.

"You want an appointment? Do I look like a fucking doctor's office and how you gonna fuck after your friend?"

"Oh please. We do it all the time; even with her piece of shit man." She said that with no type of regret.

"Hold on."

"No, she doesn't know but who cares. She's a ho so it is what it is." She shrugged and again, said it as if nothing was wrong. No wonder women always say they don't have friends. With people like her who would want any.

"I'm not making no appointments and regardless of you being a ho just like your friend, I'm good."

"A ho? Nigga, I was tryna help you out." Why was she getting mad at me calling her out like she just did her friend?

"How you helping me out?"

"Because a man usually sticks around after sex. You're leaving right away which meant it wasn't good or you have someone." Chuckling at her ignorance, I turned around and headed back to my car.

"How you fucking a bitch that's suing you?" I didn't bother to respond, got in my car and left.

See, the day I knocked Yasmina unconscious for hitting me over the head with a two by four, I left the scene. Unfortunately, in doing so, I racked up a charge to go along with the one her man had put on me for almost killing him, per his lawyer.

Anyway, I stopped by to give him an envelope that held photos of her man not only cheating on her, but with the exact friend that just propositioned me. There were also photos of him walking, dancing and affidavits of his girlfriend prostituting herself to my pops. I added the last part to be funny since she pretended like we were making shit up that night.

Long story short, in order to make the charge go away, I had to figure out a way to get Yasmina to admit that she attacked me and my reaction was self-defense. Evidently, the only witness was her man and he wasn't paying attention.

My pops lawyer was very thorough and have beaten many cases. Unfortunately, attacking her made it seem as if I did it because of her man suing me.

Also, my lawyer found out the video never came from Mya's bar but from a garage across the street. One of the cops realized there was a camera facing her bar and asked the owner for the footage. From what me and the lawyer saw, you couldn't tell it was me at first but if you zoomed in, my face was clear as day. And so was Noah Jr. laughing behind me.

Honestly, I could care less about that but when my father's

reputation and my own was on the line, decisions had to be made.

Sleeping with Yasmina wasn't ever on my mind because I did have feelings for Mya. Sadly, they had to be pushed to the side in order for me to get the truth out. Some may say there were other ways but when you have vultures who sue for anything, you had to be very sure of everything. No mistakes could be made and absolutely no distractions.

* * *

"How much longer will you be fucking that nappy headed bitch." Mya was standing outside my door when I arrived home.

"Who are you talking about?"

"That bitch who's suing you?" Moving past her to unlock my door, she barely let me use my key.

"Mya, I've told you multiple times this wasn't gonna work." Opening my door, she followed me in and closed it.

"Again, how much longer?" Tossing my keys on the kitchen counter, I went straight to my bathroom to shower. I may have cleaned myself off at Yasmina's house but a shower felt better.

As I stripped out my clothes, Mya took her shoes off and laid on the bed. Clearly, she made plans to stay here and since I'm not in a fighting or arguing mood, I didn't say a word.

"The bitch is calling you." Mya yelled from the bedroom. Instead of responding, I let the water get hotter. It wasn't much longer that I felt her hands on me.

"Mya, today—" She cut me off and wrapped both of her hands around my body to jerk me off.

"I don't give a fuck that you slept with her. It's obvious she wasn't satisfying you because if she was, I wouldn't be able to get you this way." My dick was hard as hell and she's right.

The few times Mya and I did sleep together, when we finished neither of us could stay awake. We'd fall to sleep and wash when we got up. With Yasmina, I would up and leave with no problem.

"Turn around." I said, moving her hands away.

"For what?"

"I'm about to give you what you came here for." Turning around to face her, Mya had her hands placed on the shower with her legs spread. Stepping out to grab a condom my phone was going off nonstop. Ignoring it, I got what I needed from the nightstand, and went back to handle Mya. Anything else will be dealt with later. I needed to relax and I'm positive she'll help me do just that.

Chapter Five

IVY

"Get up." I heard Noah's voice coming from the door. Rolling over, I stared at him leaning on the door to hold himself up.

"You should be in the bed." I tossed the covers off my legs and ran over to offer assistance.

"Ivy, it's been a month. I'm not perfect but I'm fine."

"I know but you still move slow." Trying to turn him around, he looked at me.

"When are you going to speak to King?" And just like that, I turned back around and went to get in bed. Noah made his way to me and sat up against the headboard.

"How are you mad at him for going off on you, for the exact thing he did to you?" I rolled my eyes.

"I'm serious. He held secrets, y'all moved past it. Now King found out about the shit you were hiding and you're mad at him. Make it make sense." Pouting like a brat, I pulled the pillow up to my chest.

"His family—"

"Don't you sit here and say his family nothing because had you been truthful, a lot of things could've been avoided." I hated that Noah was calling me out. Then again, I hated when anyone did it.

"Look, he was shot and you haven't been by to see him."

"What? When did he get shot? Is he ok?" I started panicking.

"The day your house burned down, someone called and threatened your life. King raced over there and someone shot him; twice."

"Oh my Godddd!" I covered my mouth listening as he continued.

"Someone brought out a body bag and he thought it was you." Throwing the pillow on the bed, I grabbed my towel and rushed in the bathroom to shower.

"What you about to do?" He asked when I reached in to turn the water on.

"What do you mean? I'm going to see him." Noah thought my comment was the funniest thing ever.

"Why would he wanna see the woman that held in secrets? Or the one who hasn't reached out since the fire?" I sucked my teeth.

"I'm just saying. His ex been sniffing around so don't be

surprised if you go there and she's been nursing him back to health."

"She better not be."

"It would be your own fault for disappearing." He shrugged and left me in my thoughts. Should I be worried that Stasia was there? Maybe I won't go. I turned the shower off and went to lie down.

"Nope. I'm going to see him." I spoke out loud thinking Noah was gone. He was standing outside my room.

"Be prepared to see his ex riding him or—" I slammed the door in his face and started rushing to leave.

Noah was absolutely correct about me standing in my own way. It wasn't that I didn't want to be around King, I was trying to take time to myself and gather my thoughts. My home was burned down, my man learned of the secrets I had been holding in and I was deathly afraid of miscarrying my third child.

The doctor told me to stick to bed rest if I were nervous and that's what I've been doing. However, my man was shot, his ex might be letting him fuck her from the back and honestly, I had no one to blame but myself.

The relationship with Liam was in the past but I couldn't help but feel like in a way I'm reliving it with King. The ex's showing up, doing things behind my back and not mentioning the kidnapping and ransom really bothered me.

After showering, I gathered my things to leave. It would make sense for me to contact King and let him know I was coming over; then again, I want to see if he missed me the same way I missed him. Matter of fact, it's only been a month. He shouldn't be with anyone for any reason. I guess I'll see when I get there.

* * *

"Hello. How can I help you?" A beautiful woman answered the door and I instantly felt like a loser. How could he move on so quickly and I should've called first.

"Are you ok?" The woman asked because I wouldn't respond. What was I supposed to say?

"Kingggggggg, there's some crazy woman at the door. I think she's mute." Did she just say that?

"Mute? Who the fuck is it?" I heard his voice and became agitated seeing him only in a pair of sweats and slides when he pulled the door open further.

"What's up?" He walked on his porch and closed the door behind him.

"Ugh... I was here... um... my brother said you were... never mind. I see you're ok." Stumbling over my words made him laugh.

"It's been a month since we last spoke. Now, you show up unannounced and get in your feelings when a woman opened the door. What did you stop by for?"

"To see if you were ok and since you are, I'm going to go." I stepped off the porch.

"How's my kid?" Turning around only pissed me off more because he had a smirk on his face and my body wanted him badly.

"The first appointment is tomorrow at nine." He made his way to where I was, grabbed me by the bicep and led me to the car.

"You have some fucking nerve showing up to my house after going MIA." He let go and opened the car door for me.

"Never mind the fact, you're pregnant and had you not come today, I wouldn't have known about the doctor's appointment." I put my head down in shame.

"That's our baby, Ivy." His voice was escalating.

The least you could've done was check on me but you're so got damn selfish, all you thought about was yourself."

"I'm selfish says the man that kept the kidnapping and ransom away from me." I was not allowing him to place all the blame on me.

"Exactly because it didn't happen. What would be the need for me to bring it up?"

"It doesn't matter. I should've known."

"Just like I should've known my aunt and cousin attacked you at the BBQ and made you lose our first child." I instantly went quiet.

"You didn't even bother to tell me. What if I wanted to mourn with you, huh? Shit, I just found out they threw you in the pool too." He was boiling mad at this point.

"King." I touched his arm and he moved back.

"The crazy part was you don't even see shit wrong with anything you've done or kept hidden."

"I'm sorry. They are your family and—"

"And they could've killed you. Why would you continuously hide the fact they were terrorizing you?" He started pacing the lawn.

"When Stephanie was at my house and brought up the kidnapping and ransom, why didn't you say it then. She was right there and I could've handled it." I shrugged.

"Now that I'm thinking about it, didn't you tell her to mention why you left the BBQ early. Why didn't you say it?" Again, there was nothing left for me to say.

"Fine. You want to be mad at me, ok, be mad. I deserve it." I was about to get in my car and stopped.

"Don't say shit, you're gonna regret Ivy because I can tell you right now, my tongue is vicious and every word will cut like a knife." I couldn't believe how he was acting toward me.

"Well then, I guess there's nothing left to say." I sat down and closed the door. Of course I had to roll the window down.

"Go back to your new boo thing but do not bring her to any doctor's appointments." He started shaking his head.

"That's what the fuck you worried about? The chick who answered my door."

"It's been a month so I'm not surprised."

"When you left me the first time after the party it took me weeks to find you, and yet, no other woman crossed my mind. It was about Ivy Davis, and only Ivy Davis."

"She answered the door like she lived here."

"And so what? I was talking on the phone and asked her to get it."

"Well, who was she then?" I folded my arms across my chest.

"She's my cousin who flew in from Atlanta to visit my Aunt Gloria." I felt stupid for thinking otherwise.

"Oh. I didn't know." Again, I put my foot in my mouth.

"If you think it'll only take me a month to get over you, you really don't know me at all." I knew he loved me but people do get over their lovers in a month, I think.

"King."

"Get the fuck off my property and don't come back." Those words hurt more than anything he's said to me today. I was about to say, *I'm sorry* again but the death stare he gave me, said to leave.

What have I done?

Chapter Six

KING

"That was her, huh?" Iesha asked when I stepped in the house. She was here visiting Aunt Gloria after being shot in the stomach. I was getting ready to go visit her myself since the nurse called stating she was finally awake.

Evidently, the gun used on her had hollow point bullets. It shattered her insides and because she hit her head somehow, they put her in a medically induced coma, which is sometimes common for head trauma victims. The doctor gave her the medicine to wake up last week but she never did until yesterday.

"Yup." Moving around Iesha to go in my room, I heard her call my name.

"What?"

"Are you excited about the baby?" I turned to see a grin on her face.

"You nosy as hell."

"Hell yea. When someone showed up to your house pretending to be mute, of course I'm going to listen. Matter of fact, did you investigate her background to find out if she was special needs?" I laughed hard as hell.

"I'm serious. Now a days doctors will diagnose a person with something if they don't understand things." She wasn't lying. It did feel like doctors were saying people had issues and didn't just to have them come back. That way they'll put the person on medicine and the insurance company would be paid as well. Greedy ass motherfuckers.

"Ivy is not special needs. She's just very standoffish and never been a social butterfly. You funny as hell."

"Oh, she talked to you because her lips were sealed tight."

"She thought you were my new chick." I chuckled walking away and into my room.

"I know I'm gorgeous and all but your new woman. Yuk." My cousin stuck her finger down her throat. She was dramatic as fuck at times.

"Conceited much?"

"Very. Anyway, what's the story with Stephanie?" Iesha was my uncle's daughter, my mom's and Aunt Gloria's brother.

She had four other siblings who were younger than her and into their own shit. To be honest, he wanted to take us when my mother passed but he couldn't stay the fuck outta jail. He had a hand problem when it came to women. It's exactly why Iesha's mom left him.

"Man, I don't even know." I slid my foot into the sneakers.

"Every chick I've been with she's hated and I'm not even sure why. You remember she was always fucking with Stasia." Iesha nodded her head.

It's been times we'd have parties and they'd come to visit and for some reason Stephanie would antagonize the hell outta my ex. Stasia wouldn't mention it until later and said it was family hazing. She felt if I approached my cousin, it would make her despise her even more. The situation was never as bad as it was with Ivy though. I'm quite sure it had to do with Ivy not being a fighter or the fact she didn't stand up for herself.

"Anyway, she terrorized and beat up Ivy as you know."

"Wait a minute." I snatched my keys off the dresser.

"Exactly. I've told her a few times not to let me find out she touched a single hair on Ivy and she did anyway."

"Technically she did more than touch her hair." Iesha always had jokes.

"The bitch really lost her mind coming for me." Iesha followed me down the stairs and to the car. She wanted to be there when I questioned our aunt. There's no way in hell she didn't know what was going on.

As we drove to the hospital, we spoke about her pops finally settling down. We also cracked jokes and picked up something to eat.

Pulling into the hospital parking garage, Iesha started ducking her head like the ceiling was gonna cave in. Talking about the cement to the garage was too low and they need to make them higher. We got out the car, went to the information desk to get my aunt's room number and went on about our way.

"Do you think she knows; you know?" Iesha laughed stepping off the elevator.

"Probably not since she just woke up." I opened her room door and my cousin went in first.

"Iesha? What are you doing here?" My aunt noticed her right away. Her face damn near turned white when she saw me, but why? I haven't said a thing about what I know.

"I'm here to visit you for the last time." Iesha was aware of what would take place.

"The last time? Are you moving further than Atlanta?" My aunt showed pain on her face as she sat up on the bed. She was an older woman and I'm sure the shooting took a toll on her.

"I have a few questions and we'll go from there." It was no need to beat around the bush.

"Question 1... who did this to you?" When she started to cry, I knew it was Stephanie. They weren't the perfect mother and daughter but damn, shooting her was on some hateful type of shit.

"Question 2... Why did she do it?" Iesha shook her head and sat down.

"Stephanie hated you for having new women in your life." My aunt wiped her eyes with the back of her hand.

"That doesn't make sense. King was her cousin, not her man." Iesha chimed in.

"That's what I used to say but it had nothing to do with that. Growing up, King would tell her she could be on his team. It didn't matter what the position was, she wanted badly to be a part of it." Staring out the window as she spoke, I felt a little fucked up knowing this petty ass reason was why she terrorized my women.

"Everything ok?" I turned to see a nurse checking over my aunt. She removed the monitors on her chest but kept the blood pressure cuff on. The conversation continued when she stepped out.

"When he was only sleeping with women, Stephanie didn't care. However, she saw Stasia and Ivy as competitors. I tried to tell her you'd never make them workers but she had it in her mind that you would replace her with them." Shaking my head as she continued, all I could think of was killing my cousin.

"So, she terrorized his two women for a spot on the team." Iesha couldn't believe it but with Stephanie, she didn't surprise me.

"As dumb as it may be, that's why she did it but with Ivy." I swung my head in her direction.

"She was deathly jealous of her and I don't know why. I mean she'd curse me out if you defended Ivy and called her all kinds of names. Boy was she mad when you cancelled the kidnapping and making her a worker."

"What?"

"She felt you chose Ivy over the original plan and it should've never happened." Stephanie was a piece of work but I had something waiting for her.

"How many times did you lay hands on Ivy?" It took her a few seconds to answer.

"I never hit her but I am guilty of harassing her and holding her hands while Stephanie punched and kicked her multiple times." I didn't say a word. Iesha lashed out and called her dumb as fuck.

"You didn't push her so hard she got whiplash? I mean you could've snapped her neck by how hard you did it." Aunt Gloria's head went down. I guess she forgot to add that part.

"What you failed to realize was the truth always comes out whether the people involved tell or not."

"I agree with him, Aunt Gloria. Why would you do that to Ivy?" She just met Ivy today and she was being weird thinking Iesha was my new chick. I'm sure they'll get along when properly introduced.

"I don't know. Stephanie would tell me they said things about us or did stuff that would hurt King if he found out. When I heard about her trying to kidnap Ivy for the second time." I cut her off.

"Say what?" I still had eyes on Ivy but now I needed to put more on her until my cousin was found.

"I told her it was enough. I went to my room to call 911 and she came in with her gun pointed at me." She started crying again.

"When the bullet hit me in the stomach, I bent over to grab my phone again. Stephanie hit me in the head with the gun and I can't even tell you how many times." The story was sad for someone who gave a fuck. I nodded to Iesha and watched as she stood, closed the door and waited there to make sure no one came in.

"I gave y'all everything, and I do mean everything. Instead of appreciating it y'all took my kindness for weakness and now it's time to pay the piper." My initial way to kill Aunt Gloria was to suffocate her. However, I didn't feel like wasting time as she tried to save herself by constantly trying to move the pillow or grabbing my hands. Therefore, I had fentanyl in a syringe that would go into the IV she had.

"I will always appreciate the fact you took me and Amerius in."

"King, please don't do this." I smiled at her.

"You should've never listened to your daughter. Both of y'all knew better and how I felt for Ivy; hell, Stasia too." She didn't have any words.

"Oh, and you did this." As I watched the liquid rush through the IV, a calmness came over me. This was one less person I would have to worry about trying to kill Ivy.

"I'm sorry." Were the last words she managed to get out.

KNOCK! KNOCK! I nodded to let Iesha know she could open the door. The nurse stepped in, looked at me, then my aunt and back at me.

"Let me take the IV out so if any traces of it coming back, they'll assume someone came in and gave it to her." Yup, the nurse was in on my plan from the start which was why she removed all the machines. She was paid extremely well for her services too.

"You ready?" Iesha asked, looping her arm in mine.

"Ready as I'll ever be. One down, two to go." I knew Stephanie was with Gary and like I said before, I had plans for them.

Kandy

"How you feeling?" I asked Noah. He was sitting on the couch at his house. He stayed with me for a few days when he was first shot by my ex. Once Ivy called stating she was nervous about staying alone, he went back. I've been here on the weekends helping to take care of him; not that he needed it.

"I'm good. How's Amaya?" The two of them formed a bond after he knocked Jamal out at the mall for trying to choke me to death.

"She's good. Wondering when you're taking her to the arcade for ski ball." Amaya asked him to show her how to beat me in the game. She was sticking with her story that I only beat her due to my long arms.

"Hopefully soon." He slowly stood. Jamal shot him in the stomach and the bullets splattered inside. The doctors removed everything but told him to take it easy now. Clearly, he doesn't listen because besides moving around too much, we've been having a lot of sex.

"Where's Ivy?" I asked, getting off the couch to grab him a drink.

"Upstairs depressed because King let her have it" I started

laughing. Rahasia told me some of what Amerius said happened when Ivy stopped at King's house. Iesha was cool as hell and very beautiful. I could see why Ivy made the assumption they were together but she should've asked, nonetheless.

"Let me go talk to her." Handing him the water, I took the short walk up the stairs and let a smile come over my face. Noah let me decorate his house for the most part but he did hire a decorator as well to do the other rooms and it's very nice. I'm glad his mom left him money because his father really tried to hold him hostage with it.

"Hey." I slowly opened Ivy's door. She was lying on the bed staring up at the ceiling with her hand on her stomach.

"Why you laying on the bed like you're in a coffin?" Ivy gasped with her dramatic self. I sat on the side of her.

"What's going on?" I wanted to hear her side of the story.

"King hates me." I had to laugh.

"I'm sure he doesn't but tell me why you feel that way." She turned to me. It's no secret she was naïve as hell but she did need to take responsibility for her actions.

"We had our first doctor's appointment two days ago." Ivy responded.

"Ok." She sat up.

"He didn't speak to me or ask how I was feeling. It's like he doesn't care." Staring at her for a moment made me realize Ivy was a spoiled brat just like her brother said. Not only that, Ivy could never admit when she was wrong.

"Playing devil's advocate here and I'm going off what I was told." She nodded.

"Correct me if I'm wrong. You didn't tell him about the miscarriage, the abuse, harassment, tormenting his family did, nor did you check on him when he was shot."

"I didn't know." I noticed how she skipped over everything she did.

"You may not have but if you weren't acting like a five-year-old, you would've known." I had to call out her childish behavior.

"Excuse me." She was definitely offended.

"You've been throwing tantrums lately, having disappearing acts, and lastly, you're not taking accountability for anything you've done."

"But he—"

"See, you're about to blame him for things he did to deflect what you've done." She shut right up.

"Why didn't you tell King about the doctor's appointment?" I cut her off before she could answer.

"Regardless of being angry, in your feelings or tired, that wasn't right." I could see her about to cry.

"Look Ivy." I held her hand in mine.

"King loves you; I mean really loves you." Anyone from the outside looking in could see that.

"Tuh! I can't tell. He kicked me off his property."

"As he should've because you were acting like a brat. You tried to blame him for the reason why you went MIA."

"Yea but—" Here she was trying to make up another excuse.

"You have to grow up Ivy or you will lose him."

"I already did." She pouted, throwing her hands in the air.

"That man ain't going nowhere." I rose up off the bed.

"I'm not so sure about that." I walked to the door.

"Well, if you're not, then go get him." I knew she wouldn't because she was scary and afraid of embarrassment.

"He told me in so many words not to trespass on his property."

"Then you better show up in something that'll change his mind about kicking you off again." I winked and headed downstairs. Pulling my vibrating phone out my pocket, I smiled at the person sending me a text. This was the one I had been waiting for.

"Where you going?" Noah asked. Trying to sneak out, I hit my foot on the stairs and he heard me wince.

"I'll be back shortly. If you're sleep, I know how to wake you up."

"We'll let me doze off now." He tossed his head to the side, closed his eyes and pretended to be asleep. Laughing at him, I took a deep breath. My next move was a dangerous one but it had to be done in order to live freely.

"Damn, you look sexy as hell." Jamal was excited to see me. I wore a black catsuit with some heels and a sweater wrapped around my waist.

"Hey." Moving past him standing at the door salivating over me, I stopped after seeing two other men there and a woman.

The drive was over two hours to get here and what I planned to have done in five minutes would now take longer since he had company.

The house was in a decent neighborhood from where he used to stay years back. The furniture and almost everything in here appeared to be brand new. This must be someone else's house because even when we were together Jamal was cheap and didn't want to buy anything. Hell, we slept on air mattresses and floors more than I can count.

"I assumed we were going to be alone."

"Damn, is that Kandy?" When the guy smiled, it brought back some memories. He was one of Jamal's few friends that visited in the rehab center. Then again, I wouldn't say visited when he'd take me out to his car for a quick fuck.

Crazy how at the beginning of my stay at the place, Brian's cousin worked there and would let him sign me out to satisfy his needs. In return, he would give me something to stay high. It was another reason the process took longer for me to get better. He wanted to fuck and I wanted to stay high. At the time, it was a win, win situation.

"How you been?" He hugged me tighter than what an acquaintance would and the woman noticed because she rolled her eyes at me.

"I'm good. You cleaned up nice and I must say, that body looking fierce in the catsuit." He winked and sat down on the couch.

"Don't get fucked up Brian." If Jamal only knew Brian was far from his friend.

"I'm just saying. Your baby mom looking good. What's next?" He plopped down on the couch giving me an eyesight view of the pounds of weed on the table. As I sat down, there was a duffle bag beside the couch filled with Ziplock's full of white powder. For a split second, I badly wanted to indulge.

"What you looking at?" The other unknown guy barked, scaring me.

"Don't talk to her like that." The guy stopped bagging the weed and stood toe to toe with Jamal.

"We don't know this bitch and you got her here while we doing our shit." The guy went back at him.

"She don't care. She used to get high." Jamal shrugged after blurting that out. What if I didn't want them to know that?

"Really?" He took my hand and led me in another room.

"Whose house is this?" I quizzed after glancing around the bedroom. It was decorated really nice.

"The new guy allowed me to use this spot until I found a place in Connecticut." Now that he said those words, it was a must to do what I came here for.

"Who's the new guy?" Trying to get some information out of him, I continued prying.

"You're mighty nosy." He yanked on the sweater to pull me in closer.

"Why are you being aggressive?" Smacking his hand away, he pushed me.

"Maybe it was a bad idea coming here." Trying to play innocent, I used my soft woman's voice.

I didn't want to be anywhere around Jamal, especially after

the mall incident. Unfortunately, living in fear for myself and daughter was not what I envisioned our future to look like either.

When I picked up the police report a while back after filing the restraining order, his phone number was on it. I got up enough nerve to send a message saying how much I missed him and now here we are in a room; alone.

"It wasn't a bad idea unless you didn't come to fuck." He removed his shirt.

"Jamal, I'm not here to have sex with you." Confusion was written on his face as he kicked his sneakers off.

"Oh, we're fucking for sure. See, Kandy, you gotta suck a lotta dick to make up for having me arrested and filing that restraining order on me." He moved closer trapping me in front of the closet door.

"You let that punk nigga knock me out at the movies and then, some other motherfucker waited for me at the police station and followed me. I stopped at the store and all I remember was him saying, *"Leave Kandy alone or else"* before knocking me out." He was now hovering over in just his boxers, and his breath that smelled like shit.

Noah mentioned how he had people who did certain things for him. I never asked what but I'm assuming he sent someone to get Jamal. I will reward him later for that.

"I get a call from you saying you're sorry and want to see me; of course it's to fuck. Can't no nigga do you like me." He lifted me up in his arms and literally dry fucked me against the wall.

"Put me down." I tried pushing him off but he held me tight.

"Nope. I'm about to get this first nut out and then we going round for round like we used to." It was at this very moment I realized, Jamal was high and had no idea what was really going on.

"Oh shit, Kandy. Fuck yea." After he almost dropped me, I moved away and saw white cum dripping down his leg in the flimsy boxers. I couldn't believe he really did that.

"That was good as hell. Now come here." When he turned toward the bed, I reached in my crossbody purse and grabbed the syringe. Rahasia mentioned how King killed his aunt so I figured it was the easiest way to get rid of him.

"Ahhh shit." I rammed it into his arm and pushed with all my might. I almost peed on myself when he turned around grinning.

"What the hell?" Jamal snatched me by the hair and threw me on the bed. His punches were hurting but not enough to make me stop.

"Get off me." I kicked and fought the best I could when he jumped on me.

"Why the fuck isn't the stuff working?" My heart was racing as I tried to think of something else to do. Jamal was trying his hardest to rip the front of my outfit.

"Bitch, you tried to kill me?" His words were now slurring and I finally saw him taking slow breaths. I was too nervous to touch fentanyl even though it would've been inside the syringe. What I didn't mind using was a lethal dose of cyanide. Granted, it took forever to kick in but it was starting to work.

"Get over here." He tried to grab my foot as I hopped off the bed. Lucky for me, he barely any strength left. When he started foaming at the mouth, that's when I knew it was over for him.

Watching him die gave me a sense of relief. Not only was my daughter going to be safe, so was I. His body slid down the bed and onto the floor. I used my fingers to close his eyes and got a surprise seeing Noah standing there.

"What are you doing here?" I hugged him tight. He moved me away and turned my face side to side.

"He hit you."

"I'm ok. He's gone." He hugged me again.

"How did you know where I was?" We walked out the bedroom.

"It's my job to know where you are. And besides, the woman and man are friends of mine. They're in law enforcement." What did he just say?

"Huh?" I was very confused.

"Evidently, Jamal had a long record with being arrested for drugs. The person he thought was in charge that he met up with was my boy, Trey." He pointed to the guy from the other room.

"His partner was Allison." He pointed to the chick placing handcuffs on Brian.

"Long story short, Jamal was a drug runner. He'd pick the drugs up, deliver them, get paid and do it all over again. Trey told Jamal to meet him here which he thought was Trey's house. Allison was a decoy in case you needed her."

"Excuse me." As he explained knowing about the text messages from his people, I was shocked and thankful at the same time. Since they were tapping his phone, they saw everything.

"Since you were being sneaky, I made sure to have a woman around. Things could've gone wrong and you may have needed someone to talk to after." I couldn't believe what I was hearing.

"Brian was so high; he didn't know what was going on in the other room. Therefore, he'll be arrested for Jamal's murder and the drugs that were here tonight." Noah was surprising me every word he spoke.

"Wow!"

"It's a lot to take it but it's over now. You're safe." He led me out the house.

"I may not be a street nigga but don't ever underestimate my abilities to help or keep you safe." I wrapped my arms around him and rested my head on his chest.

"I'm sorry. You're just now getting back to yourself after being shot." I felt bad that he was here and not resting.

"It doesn't matter. Even if I couldn't be there, I would've made sure you had what you needed. Well, I did anyway but you get what I'm saying." I didn't disagree with his logic because truth be told, he was right. I should've included him and I'm thankful those people did know him. Things could've gone terribly wrong with Jamal and I may not have been able to get away.

"Now, since you promised to wake me up if I were asleep when you returned, you're going to do that and a whole lot more." I laughed.

"I want you to get checked out first though." Trying to avoid a hospital visit didn't work. Noah went with me, waited and definitely had me doing some freaky things before bed. I'm just glad Jamal was a thing of the past now.

Chapter Seven

"We're definitely getting back together." I told Veronica. She came to visit me here since I'm not returning. Once King takes me back there will be no need. It's exactly why I gave up my condo and placed all my things in storage.

"What made you say that? Do you live with him and why are you staying in a hotel?" Veronica was one of those friends who tested me a lot. No matter what I said she had to have proof in her face to believe me.

We haven't been around another in a while because she moved away with her job. Our friendship wasn't what it used to be either and she's only here now for work. She asked if I knew any good places to eat in Connecticut and I mentioned being here, which was how we linked up.

"Well, when he found out about Jamaica, he softened up on me and let me kiss him in front of his girlfriend."

"Girlfriend? Bitch how y'all getting back together and he with someone?" She got on my nerves.

"Excuse me. They are not together anymore. Matter of fact, I gave him head in the hospital when he was shot. He didn't stop me and we almost had sex if the doctor didn't come in." Veronica dropped her fork.

"You mean to tell me; you told him the truth about Jamaica and he didn't kill you." I shook my head yes. Why did she go back to the previous conversation instead of focusing on me and him rekindling our romance?

"Now that, I don't believe because regardless of what took place back then, that man was in love with you. Shit, from what I heard, he planned on proposing when we got off the plane." How did she know that?

"You're lying?"

"Nope. I ran into his hating ass cousin about a week later and not only was she happy y'all broke up; she told me how devastated he was over it." Veronica shrugged.

Even though King moved away immediately, Stephanie and her aunt stayed behind to pack up their own stuff. I'm guessing he didn't want to run into me because he damn sure would have. I went straight to his house once we landed only to find him gone.

Crazy how they moved where he did and not once was I able to find them. I'm thankful as hell for social media which was how I made contact. Now Veronica mentioning that King planned on marrying me, had me upset. Yes, he said that I was supposed to be his wife, but who knew that would be the time he wanted to ask.

"As far as his new chick, what does she look like. Was she pretty, Instagram model type, what?" She stuck a fry in her mouth.

"To be honest, she's not all that—" My words were stuck in my throat when she walked in with some handsome guy.

"What?" Veronica turned around and asked who the guy was as if I'd know.

"That's the new bitch."

"Oh shit. King wasn't playing and she looks good and pregnant." Staring at the Ivy bitch, I couldn't lie and say she wasn't pretty. Honestly, her style of dress was cute, her hair was always done when we ran into one another, and I could tell she was a punk.

"How you figure? She doesn't have a stomach." I stared Ivy down just to be sure.

"She's very pretty and if she's not, she will be." Veronica laughed, sticking more fries in her mouth. The diner we were at had some really good food but I didn't come here to see this bitch.

"Not if I have anything to do with it." Tossing my napkin on the table, I stood. Veronica grabbed my wrist.

"Two things." I stopped to listen.

"If her and King are still together, he's gonna kick your ass for approaching her." I rolled my eyes. One thing about my ex, was he didn't play with anyone fucking with his woman.

"What's the other thing?"

"If they aren't together and you fuck with her, King will still kick your ass." She's probably right but if I want him back, she needs to know I'm not going nowhere.

"Why, if they broke up."

"Because from what you told me, it sounds as if he really loves her. I'm not a specialist on relationships but if you want King, let him come to you." I snatched away. I didn't tell her much besides he seemed to be smitten by Ivy. Oh, and that he claimed they were together for over a year and loved her. I guess that's enough to make an assumption. It wasn't enough to make me stop trying to get him.

"Ok. You never listened to me before. Why would you now?" She took a sip of her soda and followed me to Ivy's table. Why would she tell me not to do it but follow me?

"Well, well, well. What do we have here? Does King know you're out with another man?" Ivy lifted her head from the menu. Once she saw it was me, she rolled her eyes.

"Who the fuck are you?" The guy snapped.

"Who are you?"

"I'm—" Ivy stopped him from speaking.

"Stasia, I'm positive King gave you direct orders not to harass or even speak to me." She smiled and put the menu down.

"Direct orders. He ain't my boss." I snapped. Who did she think she was saying that to me?

"He's not my man either but you don't see me harassing you out in public." She offered me a fake smile.

"Let me guess, you broke up with him after we fucked at the hospital." I know he didn't tell her that, which was I did. She needed to be taken down off that high horse and so what if I lied about fucking. I still had his dick in my mouth.

"Stasia!" Veronica tried to grab me to move away from her table. Ivy's face was priceless; it was almost as if she wanted to cry.

"I had that dick for years and trust me, he's had this pussy." I stood in a stance and pointed at my crotch with both hands.

"Get the fuck away from this table." The guy with her stood.

"I'm going. I only stopped by to tell you no need to call or text him. We're making up for lost time."

"That's funny because they were just together at her prenatal appointment and he didn't mention you. Ain't that right Ivy?" That bitch, Kandy took a seat and made the guy sit. He was pissed. Where the hell did she even come from?

"Prenatal? The only woman King would ever get pregnant was me. I suggest you pin your bastard child on someone else."

"Bastard?" Ivy repeated me with disgust in her voice.

"Stasia, you're tripping and that shit ain't cool." Veronica pushed me back toward our table.

"Fuck her, Ivy." I heard as we sat down and looked up to see the bitch headed toward our table. The smile on my face must've aggravated Ivy because she folded her arms across her chest. Kandy walked over and stood next to her.

"Stasia, your problem should be with King, not me. I don't know you nor was I around during the time you dated."

"Hurry this conversation up. King just texted that he wanted me to stop by and ride his dick." Hell yea, I was being petty as hell.

"Good luck riding him with me on his mind." She turned around to leave.

"What would be the purpose of you on his mind when he has all this?" I stood and modeled my body.

"The same *"this"* you gave to multiple men in Jamaica one night being a whore." She used her fingers as a quote when she said the word this. Who the hell told her what happened in Jamaica anyway?

"Oh shit now." Veronica was cracking up where I was about to hook off.

"How dare you! I was drugged and raped." I yelled in embarrassment.

"Drugged and raped but allowed the man to pound you from behind while King stood there. You didn't even make him stop when your so-called man stepped in the room." She put her index finger under her chin.

"Don't sound like rape to me. It sounds like you were being a ho and got caught." When the bitch shrugged her shoulders, I lost it.

I reached around Kandy and punched Ivy in the face a few times. Before I could really get to her, someone lifted my body and literally threw me. I landed in a booth where a couple was sitting. My feet were in the air and my head hit the wall.

"Are you ok, ma'am?" The older gentleman asked. His wife had a distasteful expression.

"Honey, you know we heard her disrespecting that woman. Don't ask her nothing." I feel as black people we don't give a fuck about each other. How did my words make her not care that I was thrown around and by a man at that?

"Call the cops." Someone yelled. Struggling to get up, I saw Kandy whooping Veronica's ass. She had her in the headlock and was uppercutting the shit out of Veronica's face. I could see blood dripping down.

"Get off my friend." Still dazed from being thrown, I went to swing on Kandy and felt someone pulling my hair. I slipped on the ground and hit my head for the second time.

"This is for saying my son was a bastard." I was screaming as this bitch poured hot sauce in my face. I only knew that because she was unscrewing the damn tiny lid off the Tabasco sauce when I looked up.

"Take this." Ivy shouted and I could tell she was using all her might to shake it out. It was getting in my eyes and mouth.

I was so discombobulated; I couldn't gather up enough strength to get up. I reached out for her leg only to feel someone stepping on my arm.

"Ahhhhh!" I screamed out. My eyes were burning so I couldn't see anything.

"This is for punching me." I heard and felt a gush of water all over me. It may have been soda but it didn't come from a cup. My clothes were drenched.

"Don't ever speak negatively to me again." Ivy hit me with something else and I swear it felt as if my stomach caved in.

"I can't believe you dropped the bucket of dishes on her."

Some guy started laughing. I'm assuming it was who came with her.

"Let's go Kandy. You whooped her ass long enough." All I could do was lay there and wait for help. Oh, I'm going to get that bitch back for sure.

* * *

"Ok, you can get regular eyes drops for your eyes. There are two bald spots in your head so I prescribed some cream for you in case there were cuts from the person who attacked you." I sure did tell the doctor I was viciously attacked and I'm pressing charges. Ivy will see I'm the only one to get the last laugh.

"You have a concussion so I would advise you to take it easy. And lastly, you have a knot on your forehead and some bruising forming on your back." He handed me the discharge papers, along with the prescriptions and wished me good luck.

Snatching the papers out his hand, I went to check on Veronica. Evidently, she had to be taken away in an ambulance too.

"I'm fine. Just get me the papers to sign so I can leave." She could be heard yelling from down the hall. When I stepped in her room, she had her back turned.

"Damnnnnnn." I covered my mouth after seeing her face. She had a nose brace on, her right eye was damn near closed and she was holding an ice pack to her mouth.

"Bitch, this is your fault." She cursed, putting her shoes on.

"How was it my fault? I didn't tell you to fight Kandy. Hell,

I could've told you that bitch fight like she in a championship trying to get a belt." When Kandy fought me at Ivy house that day, she almost did me the same as she did Veronica had Ivy not sprayed us with the water hose. Her punches felt like bricks against your face.

"I told you to leave Ivy alone but nooooo, you had to keep going."

"The bitch tried me by saying—"

"No one cared what she said but you. Then, you speak ill of her kid. What the hell was wrong with you?" She waited for me to answer.

"I'm telling you right here and right now, if I run into King somehow and he asked me what happened, I'm telling."

"Really?"

"Hell yea, really. I love my life but clearly you don't love yours." She shoulder checked me on the way out.

"Veronica." I called out.

"Leave me the fuck alone right now and don't call me. If I want to talk, I'll reach out to you." She stormed off after taking the papers from the nurse who stopped her. Following behind, I stayed in the cut after seeing a G wagon pull up. Some dude jumped out the truck and his face was terrifying.

"What the fuck happened to you?" He hugged her when she started crying.

"I told you to leave that bitch alone." Was he talking about me? She must've been whispering but he damn sure wasn't. I wonder what she told him.

"Where she at?" I hid some more so he wouldn't see me. I'll fight a chick anytime, but not no man.

"We're getting married in a couple of months. Ain't no way in hell my fiancé supposed to look this way." He opened the passenger door and helped her in. Did he say they were getting married? Why didn't she tell me?

After kissing her lips, he took one last look and that's when I noticed exactly who he was. How the fuck did she end up with the guy from Jamaica?

"Excuse me." I turned to see a young girl walking out. Instead of going out that door, I decided to call a cab and have it meet me out front. I'm not sure if Veronica's man was lurking and I'm not trying to find out.

"Ma'am, I'm glad you're still here. The detective returned to take your statement on the attack." I'm outta here soon as I tell him what took place and I'm going to add to it just because. Ivy will learn not to fuck with me.

Chapter Eight

IVY

"Hi, how can I help you?" I heard Maria at the front door. I've been staying here and at Noah's house.

When the fire first happened, this was the last place I wanted to be. However, Kandy was over my brothers a lot and those two were always acting like newlyweds. One time Kandy came in the kitchen dressed only in a short T-shirt barely covering her butt. She apologized because it was the middle of the night and I'm usually in bed.

I wasn't upset but it did put things in perspective for me about Noah. He finally found a good woman and I was happy for him. He deserved it after everything he'd been through and all the weight he carried over the years none of us knew about. Kandy brought out the good in him and it constantly showed.

When you factor in Amaya, they were really a cute, blended family.

"I'm Detective Simmons. Does Ivy Davis reside here?" Hearing my name made me rush over to the door.

"I'm Ivy."

"No she's not. Give us a minute." Maria closed the door in his face. He started to knock again.

"What is wrong with you? Never admit to being the person they're looking for when you don't the reason they're here."

"Maria, I haven't done anything. It's obvious they're here for something else." She remained in front of the door for a minute.

"Ay Dios mio." Her hands went up.

"It's fine Maria." She rolled her eyes. I opened the door and the detective was ready to knock again.

"How can I help you, Detective? I'm Ivy Davis."

"You've been a hard person to find." He explained how he went to my home and saw it was burned to the ground. He also went to my job as well. Someone with a big mouth told him I was taking a leave of absence. It wasn't a secret, yet it wasn't for anyone to tell either.

I didn't have to work once it came to light that my mother left all three of us money. However, I did enjoy getting up each morning to go. It gave me a sense of independence and free, yet I still felt the need to be a loner.

"Why were you looking for me?" I asked and noticed a cop car pulling in.

"Three days ago you were caught on camera being attacked by a woman." That was true but why was he here.

"You, in return assaulted her back by yanking her hair, tossing a bucket of heavy dishes on her and evidently, tossed tobacco sauce in her face." I didn't say a word.

"Unfortunately, I'm here because we have to place you under arrest."

"What? You just said the camera showed her attacking me first." A woman cop stepped in to place me in handcuffs.

"The woman in question filed charges against you, and she was charged as well. If you would like to do the same, we can talk about it at the station."

"What's going on here and why is my daughter in hand-cuffs?" My father barked coming down the stairs.

"Daddy it's ok." I had to face the repercussions of my actions. It felt extreme when I was defending myself but it was no need to fight it.

"It's not ok for the cop to be pushing a woman outside her own house while she's pregnant." The cop and detective stopped.

"I'm sorry. I didn't know you were expecting." The woman seemed sympathetic.

"Exactly and you have yet to read her, her rights. Therefore, this arrest has already been deemed illegal if you ask me."

"Sir, we have to get her in the car first and then she'll be read her rights." The detective attempted to be nice as the cop walked me outside.

"Do you think I'm a fucking idiot?" My father caught all of us by surprise saying that.

"No Sir, I do not." The woman cop responded, opening the door.

"Then you know as well as I, that once you place someone under arrest, you immediately read them their rights." No one said a word.

"I suggest you remove those cuffs and let your boss know we'll be down with our lawyer shortly." The officer didn't want to remove the cuffs.

"Do I need to make a call to Captain Bluford or Mayor Stanford?" The cop and detective looked at one another.

"She needs to be there today." It seemed as if my father got aggravated each time the detective spoke.

"Take them off." The officer finally let me free and I ran straight to my father. I heard a car door opening behind me and soon after they pulled off. I wanted to turn around but then again, there was no need.

"Thank you." I backed away to go in.

"Get yo ass in the house and clean your face. Snot tricking down your nose and the mascara must be cheap because it's staining your face." He couldn't be nice for one minute.

"Noah Sr." Maria yelled.

"Don't Noah Sr., me. She looks fucking disgusting." He wiped his shirt off making me even more embarrassed.

"I bet you'll listen next time I tell you not to do something." Maria chastised me on the way to the bathroom. Who would have thought Stasia would file charges on me? I guess the diner people called the cops when we left because there wasn't any on scene. And why didn't they arrest Noah?

"Where is King? Why haven't you spoken his name since you been here? Did you piss him off?" I sucked my teeth at Maria already thinking it was my fault we weren't talking.

"Evidently, King had sex with his ex when he was shot." I wasn't about to explain what we went through. There was no point since he ran to Stasia.

"I don't believe that and you shouldn't either." After cleaning my face and looking in the mirror, I wanted to cry again just because.

"It was at the hospital." Turning around, Maria hugged me tight.

"Before you believe what she said, go ask your man."

"He's not my man." I grabbed tissue to wipe my nose again.

"Ivy, let's go." My father shouted from the living room. We were in the downstairs bathroom.

"I'm coming." He was standing at the door.

"Let's get this shit over with and when we're done, you're going to look at some houses." It was early afternoon and I had planned on staying in all day.

"But—"

"But nothing. You're a grown ass woman who needs to deal with her problems." Was he really saying deal with the arsonist who burned my house? Or Stasia who attacked me then went to the police?

"Daddy."

"Fuck the bitch who pressed charges and that man. You need to be alone for a while to figure out your life." I thought my life was pretty much put together, then once King's ex came around, we started falling apart.

"All this running back and forth from my house to your brother's is childish." I thought he was done talking.

"Grow up Ivy; you're about to be a mother to my grand-child. He or she will need a stable home so get it together." He opened the door just as Mr. Bean pulled the car around. I begged Maria to come, but she declined and said that's what I got for not listening when she told me to be quiet. Getting in the car, I sat opposite my dad in the Bentley.

"Ivy, I'm getting older and I don't want to die knowing you're out here acting like a kid." I turned to stare out the window.

"Maria told me that man loves you. Why are you hiding from him?"

"It's a long story."

"Well, we have twenty minutes. Get to talking." My father lived far from the town which was why it would take longer getting there.

After telling him as much as possible, he still said I needed to grow up, apologize and get my man. Hearing those words come from him made me smile. I wonder if this was a start to a new daddy, daughter relationship for us. The car stopped in front of the jail.

"When we get in here don't open your mouth unless me or

the lawyer tell you too." I agreed, stepped out and let him take the lead.

* * *

"The bitch pressed charges on you?" Noah thought it was hilarious. I was at his house because after the fight him and my father had, he refused to return for any reason.

When we got to the jail, the captain was waiting for us. Him and my dad greeted one another and he apologized for the actions of the detective and cop. It wasn't that they weren't supposed to bring me down: it was more that they didn't read me, my rights. If this was to come up at court, the case would be thrown out right away.

"Why didn't she tell on you?" I questioned, pouring a glass of milk. This pregnancy had me eating and drinking the weirdest things.

"She doesn't know who I am would be the only reason I can think of." I gulped down the milk and poured another. The detective did tell us they weren't looking for the guy or other two women because it was no need when they had me and Stasia. It didn't make sense to me or my father, but we let it go because it was Noah and Kandy. There was no need to bring them into it.

"Damn, Ivy. You're drinking up all the milk." I rolled my eyes.

"Anyway, daddy had his realtor meet me when we left the

jail. He showed me a few places, including one that's two streets over from here."

"Good. Now when you're in trouble I won't have far to go." I tossed the dish towel at him.

"I'm serious. You're always in something." He joked, answering his ringing phone. I finished the glass of milk and left him alone to speak privately to whoever called. A few minutes later he took a seat next to me on the couch.

"So, I'll be gone for a few weeks." I turned the television down.

"Where are you going and I'm coming?" He laughed.

"To a rehabilitation facility."

"What? Really? Noah, I'm so proud of you. Wait! Why are you doing it now?"

"It's time and Kandy won't give me an heir if I'm a fiend." I almost used the bathroom on myself from laughing.

"As long as you're doing it for yourself, I'm happy." He rested his head on the couch.

"She'll be here to keep you company if you want. Try not to get into any fights because you know she'll get involved."

"I'm appalled." He turned to me.

"Kandy loves you like a sister and so does Rahasia and Mya. Ivy, you can open up and be friends with them."

"I know. I'm just used to being alone."

"Well, you don't have to be." I reached over to grab my vibrating phone off the coffee table. I looked at Noah.

"It's time to talk to him, Ivy." He was right. King and I needed to have a conversation. I kissed his cheek and went to my bedroom here. There were so many questions I had to ask but none of it mattered when he sent a text asking me to come outside. When I opened the door, he was standing outside his truck on the phone.

"Let's take a ride." With no questions asked, my ass hopped right in.

Chapter Nine

NOAH

I was happy King called Ivy because they needed to talk. She was upset that he wasn't speaking to her and from what he told me, he was in search of his cousin, Stephanie. He was checking on Ivy through me, Kandy and Rahasia. His ex was trying her hardest to get him back, yet and still he only wanted my sister.

I admit it shocked me that King called. We don't have a friendship or called ourselves acquaintances. However, when it came to Ivy, we were on the same page about her safety.

To say he was mad about what took place at the diner was an understatement. His security told him, we were at the restaurant but because he didn't come in, he had no clue about the incident inside. When we left, so did he. Therefore, the guy never witnessed the cops coming either.

Anyway, I explained what happened and after we laughed about Ivy pouring the Tabasco sauce and dropping dishes on Stasia, we agreed Ivy needed to be extra careful with the pregnancy. King wanted the baby just as much as my sister. He vowed to keep her safe the best he could and I planned on holding him to it; especially now that I've committed to this rehab shit.

It shouldn't have taken me this long and to be honest, the only reason I'm going was because of Amaya. Of course, I would've eventually but after careful consideration and all the talks she and I had, it was time. That little girl had a hold on me and she knew it. Kandy did too.

"Hey, Babe." I was upstairs getting ready to pack. Kandy walked in the house about an hour after Ivy left.

"Hey." She walked over to kiss me.

"I packed your bag already." She went to my closet and drug out two duffle bags.

"This bag has all your clothes, pajamas, socks and boxers. The other one has your toiletries, a few pair of sneakers, some crossword puzzle books and your work laptop is in your brief-case." I chuckled because you're not supposed to bring any technology to the rehab.

However, since it's an expensive ass place, they pretty much allowed you to do whatever as long as you followed the program to a T.

"What would I do without you?"

"Be lonely." She shrugged, removing the other bag off the bed. It only had socks inside so far.

"I'm proud of you, Noah and your mom would be too. Hell, he may not say it but I'm sure your father will be." I ignored the last part.

"I understand your frustration with him and I'd never tell you to speak to him. But you have to let that anger and hurt go. It's only going to consume you and since we're getting married and having six kids, it's time for you to be happy. Well, Amaya makes seven but you get what I'm saying.

"Married? Six kids?"

"I've told you on plenty of occasions that you're mine for life. In my mind, we're already married and once you've completed the program, we can work on the first baby." I pulled her in front of me.

"Outta all the women I've had sex with, you are the only one who made wanna do better."

"That's because I'm the shit." We shared a laugh.

"I'm serious. You and Amaya are just what I needed. I wish my mother could've met you." I moved a piece of hair out her face.

"If she was anything like you, I'm sure I would've loved her too." We started kissing until her phone rang. Amaya called to say her grandmother wouldn't let her eat chocolate and she earned it. Listening to Kandy speak to her daughter told me, I made the right choice with her.

"Now, don't let none of those women get you or her a beat down." She put her phone on the nightstand and stripped.

"With all this, why in the hell would I risk it?" Kandy pulled my sweats down and gave me some explosive ass head. Shit, it took me a few minutes to get myself together after releasing. We ended up having sex and showering right after.

Reaching under the pillow, I felt for the velvet box. I planned on asking for her hand in marriage when she dropped me off at rehab and changed my mind after that performance.

She was worried about me getting enticed by other fiends, and I was worried about other men tryna take her from me. Kandy needed to be my fiancé right away.

"Kandy." She was getting in the bed. The drive to the place was an hour away but my time to be there was eight. It was already after midnight and we were both tired.

"Yea, Babe." She pulled the covers up and laid on her side. I went to where she was, got on one knee and opened the box. The ring was pretty big if I say so myself, but I damn sure kept the receipt. If she doesn't accept this proposal that shit going back immediately.

"I love you with everything I have. Will you marry me?" Tears were racing down her face.

"Are you sure, Noah?" Now why would she question my proposal when she just said we were getting married and having six kids?

"I've never been more sure of anything in my life." She said yes and started doing that hysterical, can't catch your breath type of cry when I slid the ring on.

"I love you so much Noah." We kissed and as much as I wanted to have more sex, I needed to sleep.

Going in the bathroom, I locked the door, grabbed my

dope and snorted a few lines. I tried not to ever get high when Kandy was around but since this was officially my going away party for myself, I indulged.

Getting in the bed after flushing any remaining drugs down the toilet, I turned over and felt Kandy grab my hand.

"Did you get rid of it all?" And here I thought she had no idea.

"Yup."

"Good because I planned on tearing this place up to find all of it. I didn't want it here when you came home and have you relapse."

"It's going to be hard, I'm not gonna lie." She turned over.

"Very hard but I'll be here to help you." She pecked my lips and snuggled up as close as has could get. It wasn't much longer before we both dozed off.

* * *

BEEP! BEEP! The alarm going off made both of us groan. It felt as if we just went to sleep.

"Can we sleep in for a few more minutes?" Kandy whined, climbing on top of me.

"I don't have to go so I'm down." Pulling the covers over us, she quickly jumped out the bed.

"The sooner you get this done, the better." I agreed but still took my time getting up.

We ended up having a quickie in the shower because she

said, we needed to celebrate our engagement. I didn't mind but, in my opinion, she wanted to make sure there was no need for me to seek sex elsewhere. I told her when she came to visit, we could fuck in the car; I even told her to rent a U-Haul van and put an air mattress in it.

Needless to say, we left the house to grab breakfast before hitting the road. We held hands like two teenagers for the entire ride. Kandy wanted to be as close as possible and since she couldn't sit in my lap on the drive there, that's what she wanted to do.

"Ok we're here." Kandy got out first, leaving me inside the car to gather my thoughts. Did I really want to do this? Was I going to be able to stay clean? What if I relapse? With so many things running through my mind, I didn't notice Noah Sr. standing in front of my car with Maria and Mr. Bean. My car door opened and Kandy was standing there waiting for me to get out.

"Babe, try an stay calm ok."

"Did you know he was coming?" She slammed her hands down on her hips.

"Now how would I, the crackhead, know he was coming? We don't like each other." I had to crack a smile. She was right, her and my father despised one another.

"Oh, Noah. I'm so proud of you." Maria hugged me. She said Ivy was at the house and wanted to come but had morning sickness. I guess that's who told them about today.

"Make us proud Noah." Mr. Bean hugged me too. My

father stood there giving me the evil eye. Instead of entertaining him, I grabbed my bags out the trunk.

"I'm going to miss you, Babe." Kandy wrapped her arms around my neck.

"You know I can't use the phone for the first two weeks." The facility wanted me to focus on myself.

I chose this particular spot because they were highly recommended. I was going cold turkey and this was the best place for that. I didn't want to be on methadone and I'm not knocking anyone who does; it's just not for me. Once I'm done, that's it.

"I knowwwwwww." She whined.

"Are you two going inside together?" My father spoke as I walked past.

"No we're not old man and if I were, is there a problem." Kandy sassed, standing in front of him.

"I just figured two fiends would get cleaned together." I turned around.

"Noah Sr., I've come to the realization that you like the negative attention. You want me to respond so you can say nasty things to me. But guess what." My father stared at her.

"What? And you better not say you never did drugs."

"I enjoy being around you too." Kandy blew him a kiss and he pretended to gag. What old man acted like him?

"What you want?" I was at the door getting ready to go in. My plan was to wait until the last minute but with my father here it's best to go in right away.

"What the—?" My father hugged me tight and pushed me away.

"I'm proud of you, Son and your mom would be too." He waved me off.

"Noah Sr., you're going to make me cry. That was beautiful." Maria was teary eyed.

"Get your crying ass in the car. This was the reason I said you shouldn't have come. Always with the theatrics." Those two went back and forth.

"Thanks, Pops. I appreciate that." I gave Kandy one last kiss and hugged her tight. It was going to be a long two weeks but with her waiting for me, it would be worth it.

"Oh, guess what Noah Sr.?" I had no idea what Kandy was about to say.

"What you want now? You should be going inside." He just couldn't help himself.

"How can I when there's a wedding to plan. Guess who's going to be your daughter in law." When she kissed his cheek, and he swung that stupid cane at her he don't really need, I laughed hard as hell.

"When you have my grandkid it better not be on drugs."

"The baby won't be but I'm gonna bother you every day for the rest of my life now. Can I call you, Father, Dad..." Her voice trailed off following behind him to be smart.

"Get away from me you damn gnat. You're like a fly that won't leave me alone." He kept trying to swing that cane but she would run around him.

"I'd say your dad will have his hands full with her as a daughter in law." Maria was shaking her head.

"Wait until he meets her daughter, Amaya. She's the one who will really get on his nerves." Maria looked at me.

"Your father always wanted grandkids so even if she does, he'll pretend that she's not." We hugged.

As my father went to the car with Mr. Bean and Kandy antagonizing him, I had to smile. I was getting clean and had a woman in my life who didn't leave when times got rough. What more can I ask for?

Chapter Ten

KING

"**W**hat happened at the diner and don't leave anything out." I asked Ivy. She was at her brother's house. I could've had her stay with me but I was in and outta town with work and searching for Stephanie. Iesha would've kept her company at my house. However, she assumed that was my new girlfriend and knowing Ivy, she'd probably make it weird.

As she explained what took place and what Stasia said, I had to tell her the truth. I planned on mentioning the hospital scene regardless and just like I told Amerius, Stasia would make it her business to tell Ivy just to hurt her.

"Did you sleep with Stasia?" She asked again since I didn't answer the first time.

"No." It was partly the truth.

"She was very adamant about you two having sex and how you're waiting for her to ride you." Ivy told me more of what she said.

"Why are we here?" I pulled up in front of her father's house. Turning the car off, I let my seat go back as far as possible and stared at Ivy. I was very much in love with this woman and I knew my next set of words were going to hurt her for sure.

"In the hospital, Stasia told the staff she was my woman. They allowed her in the room and yes, she did go down on me." Ivy gasped.

"My shoulder and abdomen were bandaged up and no matter how much I tried to stop her, she continued. Before you ask, yes, she was able to make me cum." Ivy turned her face up.

"I had planned on relaying that information to you, but she beat me to it."

"Why didn't you say anything when I stopped by your house?" She started crying and it bothered the fuck outta me to know Stasia had one up on her. It didn't matter that it was against my will. The fact she could hurt Ivy fucked with me.

"You mean the day you assumed Iesha was my girl. That was the same day you slipped up and told me about the doctor's appointment." She opened her mouth and closed it right back.

"Look, we're about to have a baby and I don't want you upset."

"Do you love her?" I ran my hand over my head like most men do when they're thinking of what to say.

"She was the woman, I planned on marrying at one point. Do I love her? I wouldn't say love, more than I cared for her." Stasia *and I were together longer than me and Ivy. Of course there would be some sort of feelings there.*

"Ok. We can co-parent and please don't take the baby around your cousin or aunt." Ivy opened the door to get out. I stopped her by grabbing her arm.

"Stephanie shot my aunt in the stomach." I wasn't going to tell her because she'll assume I'm next.

"Oh my goodness. Are you ok?" I loved how she worried about me no matter how upset she was.

"I'm fine because I'm the one who actually took her life and I will do the same to

Stephanie." Ivy sat there in utter disbelief. I stepped out the car, went to her side and helped her out.

"This is the safest place for you right now. Do you understand?" She nodded.

"Do not leave here without one of your brothers or me." She remained quiet as I walked her to the door.

"Stephanie will try to find you and use you as bait to get me. Take heed to what I'm saying." I made her look at me.

"So I'm stuck in the house?" She pouted.

"Until I find her, yes. In the meantime, Stasia will be the least of your concern. Now go inside and take care of our baby." I kissed her cheek and waited until she closed the door.

That was the last time we laid eyes on one another. Kandy and Rahasia were now my go to when it came to keeping tabs on Ivy.

"You sure you're ready to do this? I can take over and tell

you what happened." Amerius asked taking me out my thoughts, regarding the task ahead of us.

"I'm positive. Did Rahasia pick Ivy up for that fake ass slumber party?" Rahasia was trying to keep Kandy sane since Noah went to rehab. She decided having a girl's night would be fun. I asked her to invite Ivy and I'm glad she did.

"Yea they just got home from the store. I told her don't be using my money to buy a whole bunch of crap for Ivy. Her pregnancy eating habits are yours. Matter of fact, I'm sure she did anyway so give me a hundred dollars."

"Nigga, Ivy ain't buy no hundred dollars' worth of grocery for the weekend."

"You have to incorporate lights, water, gas—" I ignored his stupid ass and continued grabbing what I needed.

"Make sure you tell Ivy how you're tryna extort me for money."

"Whatever." He waved me off like the punk he was. Him and Ivy were kinda close now so I knew he wouldn't say that shit to her.

"Let's go." I locked up, hopped in my car and headed to one of my last jobs. There was still work to do but at least this part would be done and over with.

* * *

"Yes King. Oh shit. I'm cumming baby." Stasia moaned out as I leaned on the door inside her hotel room. She was so engrossed on getting herself off, she had no idea I was here.

"Feel good."

"What the hell?" The light from outside was shining on her but she couldn't see me at first. She turned the light on and rushed to pull her shorts up.

"How did you get in here?" Ignoring Stasia's question, I stepped further in the room, placed one of my hands behind her neck and forced her off the bed.

"What's going on?" Grabbing her phone, I slammed my foot on her back making her face hit the ground. I erased the entire thing not caring about whatever she had on it.

"When I lift up my foot, you're going to stand and go in the other room." Without another word she nodded.

"Amerius." He was getting things together for me.

"What's up Stasia? You finished getting off on my brother?" As he laid the rope next to the chair, I pushed her down in it.

"King, she was talking shit." She cried out before anything happened.

"Oh, so you know exactly why I'm here." It's no secret that Ivy was part of the reason Stasia would lose her life tonight.

"Can I explain?" I pulled up a chair to sit in front of her. She stayed in a suite that had a living room and kitchen. It was rather nice if I say so myself.

"Shhhh." I quieted her down for the moment. Crossing my legs, I stared at her like a child about to get scolded by the principal.

"Let's talk about what happened in Jamaica." I learned so much about that trip and I wasn't even there.

"Jamaica?"

"That's why you returned, right. To tell me that you were drugged and raped." She swallowed hard.

"Walk me through what happened." I circled my index finger in the air to make her start talking.

"King."

"Walk me through what the fuck really happened." Tears began to fall because she knew I found out the truth.

"The girls brought some guys to the villa and—" As she kept up with the original lie about being raped, I allowed it just to see if at some point she'd spill the truth.

"I swear that's what happened." I nodded and uncrossed my legs. Placing my elbows on my knees, I made direct eye contact with her.

"Let me tell you the truth about Jamaica since you can't find the right words to do so." Amerius was shaking his head.

There was a knock at the door but I told him to have the people wait outside for a few minutes. Stasia needed to hear what I knew without interruptions.

"I'm gonna give you the short version. Is that cool?" Stasia said nothing.

"You went to Jamaica with your friends and had a great time. Y'all did the excursions, went to a few clubs and ate out every night. Does that sound about right?" She agreed.

"Good. We're on the same page." Standing up, I grabbed a cup from Amerius and let him pour me a shot of Henney that we picked up on the way here. Whenever we did a job that required me to be longer than expected, I'd take a few to keep me calm.

"The night you were allegedly drugged and raped, your friends invited some guys over." She nodded.

"The thing was, one of those same guys had been hanging out with you the entire week unbeknownst to Veronica and Sam." Her eyes grew wide. I had Amerius pour me another shot.

"Yea, you and the one dude flirted the first day y'all met and continued to spend time together out there." Veronica and Sam stayed in separate villas so they weren't aware of the sneaky shit Stasia was doing.

"King, he was the tour guide." I chuckled at her trying to maintain some part of the lie.

"The last night there, you and him made plans to link up but you never told Veronica or Sam. And it was you who spiked their drinks before the guys came over."

"You ain't shit for drugging your friends." Amerius barked making her jump.

"The dude asked if you would do a threesome beforehand and being that you agreed, you had to make sure your girls were so fucked up they wouldn't know it happened, or how much you enjoyed it."

"That's not true. I would never do that to them." I couldn't believe the way she was carrying on about not being responsible for her friend's almost dying. Whatever she gave them was she overdid it. Now if anyone was raped and drugged it was those two.

"Veronica and Sam were rushed to the hospital because of overdosing. You tried to pretend as if you didn't know, which was why you returned days later. You and the one guy you were messing with was arrested. What you didn't know was, Veronica was creeping with one of the guys on my team. He was in Jamaica when all of this happened." Amerius opened the door and in walked Veronica and Alvin.

Stasia didn't know him well because he worked in California with Amerius but when he met Veronica on a visit, he ended up traveling monthly to see her. She would go see him as well until he packed up and moved with her.

Again, something Stasia didn't know because they weren't in contact as much after the Jamaica trip. Veronica walked over and smacked fire from Stasia. She jumped up and Alvin placed a gun directly on her head. Veronica cursed her out for a minute but I had to push both of them away because I wasn't done.

"And last but not least, when you showed up at my building with all that information from your private investigator, I had to laugh because you went through a lot to make the lie believable."

"How would I get all that information if it wasn't true? King, someone told you a lie." All I could do was shake my head. Stasia was caught, yet kept going with the story.

"You found that man, gave him all those photos, had him change Veronica's medical record to yours, and even went as far as sending him a photo of Stephanie and Darryl to make it appear that they were there too." At this point nothing else needed to be said.

She paid that man hella money and it took him a while to

get everything perfect for her. He wasn't too happy Stasia had him involved in her shit because he too, lost his life.

"What's so crazy about the entire story was, that nigga you fucked admitted dialing my number from your phone as you were fucking. Evidently, you and him slept together the night before but didn't tell anyone." The tears kept falling as I replayed word for word what the guy said.

"From what he said before slicing his throat, he said you mentioned not having a man an wanted to sleep with him since it was Hedonism. You spoke about me when you were drunk though, which made him go in your phone and call me. Oh, he thought it was funny." I always told Stasia to keep her phone locked and she never listened. I bet she wished she did now.

Me and Alvin went to Jamaica when Stasia first showed up with those photos. It was a weekend trip but he knew where the guy lived since he had family there. Running down on that nigga had him telling the entire story.

Evidently, he sweet talked women to do crazy shit like that all the time when they visited. In my eyes that's a form of premeditated rape. Therefore, his ass had to go. No woman on vacation would have to worry about him or his friends again.

"I didn't want you to leave me for being experimental."

"That would've happened for sure but instead of facing that, you lied and now you're about to die for it."

"Please don't do this."

"What you should've done was said we needed a break before you went. At least you fucking two niggas wouldn't have been bad. All you thought about was yourself and now you will suffer consequences." I had Amerius pass me a thick paid or gloves.

"King, think about what we shared. My name is still on your chest. Please don't do this."

"Actually, I covered that shit with fire. You know my woman Ivy, who's about to have my baby was tattooed over my back. You wanna see." I turned and lifted my shirt to show a head shot of Ivy. It was freshly done too.

Ivy didn't know about it yet because I picked her up from Noah's and dropped her off at her father's. Rahasia mentioned Kandy trying to spend each day with Noah before rehab so I got her out the house.

"No. No. You can't love anyone but me." She was shaking her head and crying hysterically.

"Your mother sent her regards before taking her last breath." Amerius handed me the metal can.

"Please tell me, you didn't kill her."

"I didn't. You did when you continued fucking with Ivy." I shrugged and waited for Alvin to place duct tape on Stasia's mouth. He told Veronica to go in the other room and close the door. What I'm about to do would have Stasia screaming and people calling the cops.

"Without further ado." I removed the lid off the can and poured the liquid on Stasia's leg and smiled as it ate threw her skin. The muffled screams didn't bother me at all.

As the acid tore through her body it felt good knowing my past would no longer bother my future. Stephanie was up next.

Chapter Eleven

STEPHANIE

"I can't believe my mother really died from the gunshot." I paced back and forth in the tight ass motel room talking to myself. This was beneath me but there was nothing I could do to change it.

Any money I had in the bank was removed, credit cards were closed and we even had to ditch the car. We found a buy here, pay here that took my brand-new Mercedes truck and downgraded me to a damn Ford Escape. I have never in my life been in a small car like that.

If that wasn't bad, Gary was a lazy fuck who didn't want to do shit but eat and sleep all day. He even brought his damn PlayStation along for something to do. While I'm figuring out ways to leave this area, he was trying to find ways to maneuver through some got damn Spider-Man game.

The money we did have in a duffle bag was starting to dwindle down. Between eating, ordering on Instacart for groceries and using gas to drive back and forth to stakeout Ivy at her father's house, I had to devise a plan and fast.

In my mind, King should've been dead and gone by now, and would be if Gary didn't push me that night.

"You're the one who shot her for getting ready to reach out to King. You could've just left her there. I mean by the time he found out, you would've been gone anyway." I swung my head in Gary's direction. Who told him to say anything? If at any point I thought I'd be able to whoop his ass, I would've done it.

"Whatever." As bad as I wanted to curse him out, I didn't. Truth be told we needed one another to get away.

"I'm taking a shower and then going for a drive."

"Good. I need some fresh air." Picking up my towel to go in the bathroom, Gary stepped in behind me.

Lately, we turned to one another sexually. What else could we do? Neither of us felt the need to pay outside people for sex so why not. In my eyes, Darryl was way better than him. Yet and still, we took turns pleasing one another.

When we finished, we threw on disguises to leave the room. The new ones were more my style and I felt no one would ever recognize us. However, his dumb ass picked up a hat with long dreads going down his back. He looked stupid as fuck but that was on him.

"We have to stop by Liam's apartment first." He was the one keeping us up to date with what he heard King was doing.

At first, he wanted nothing to do with me. He had the

audacity to blame me for my cousin almost killing him. I told Liam it was his fault for not getting over Ivy, knowing he was telling the truth about it being my fault. Anyone associated with me, King was getting rid of.

My two friends and their families were found murdered at different locations. The only reason Liam was still alive was because King had him upside down dying from what he said. His only choice was to tell on me in order to save him and his mother's life. I get it but he should've taken that L instead of saying my name.

"For what? He already pledged his allegiance to your cousin." Gary whined getting in the car.

"What do you mean, why? He has my money at his house." It was a little over a hundred thousand, and it was mine and I wanted it. Whatever Liam does after was his business.

"Stephanie, you don't think King had someone watching his house. And why would Liam contact you out the blue for your money?" What he said made sense but why would King watch Liam's house? We never met over there because he lived with his mother and he told me she was mean. If anything, my cousin would be watching my house to see if I'd go there. Gary can be mad all he wanted, I'm getting my money and that's that.

On the drive over, Gary complained about everything he could possibly think of. The truck was too small, he was missing his time on the PlayStation, why didn't I stop for food, etc. It was annoying as hell and after we get back, I'm leaving him right there. Not being able to roam freely was one thing, but having to listen to him complain was enough to drive me insane.

"I'll be right out." I parked the car outside Liam's house, checked my baseball cap that had a long weave hanging down and fixed the schoolteacher glasses. I could resemble a nerd easily.

"Hurry up." I gave him the finger getting out. Keeping my head down, I went to the door and knock loud and quick. A woman answered looking as if she just woke up.

"Yes. How can I help you?"

"Hi, I'm here for Liam." She stared for a moment.

"Liam, some new bitch is here to see you."

"Bitch? You don't even know me." I rolled my eyes and tried to relax. There was no need to cause a scene out here. The plan was to come and go but his mother made it hard not to wanna bash her face in.

"Send her in." He shouted in the background.

"Hell no. The only female allowed in here unattended was Ivy and you fucked that up." She let a grin creep on her face. I noticed Liam limping behind his mother.

"Come on." He took my hand in his.

"I'm tired of all these different ho's coming over." She slammed her door.

"Don't mind my mom. She was team Ivy." I snatched my hand out of his.

"I'm only here for my money. No need to bring up that bitch name."

"Damn, you really despise a woman who has done nothing

to you." I folded my arms across my chest when we got in his room. It was true, Ivy Davis did nothing to me except exist. She made my cousin fall in love, who in return forgot about me.

"I know you're still in love with her but my cousin won't let you have her. And besides, she didn't fuck you like me so there was no competition." I don't even know why the sex part was brought up.

"You still mad I called her name when we were fucking?" He thought it was funny where I wanted you to shoot him in the head. That's one of the most disrespectful things a man can say to a woman during sex. Lifting a duffle bag out the closet, he handed it to me. It was a little heavy, but I guess it would be with that much money in it. I only left it there because after clearing the safe out at my house, he called ne over for sex. I was nervous about leaving it in my car that night and told him it was my clothes.

"Good luck." Walking out his room quickly, his mom stopped me at the door.

"I know you're the one who had my son caught up in your shit. Had him tortured by that crazy motherfucker because you wanted to go rogue." It was obvious Liam ran his mouth.

"What are you talking about?"

"Don't ever come back to this house again. You're not welcomed here." She opened the door.

"I'll only return if any of my money is missing. And if it's even a dollar short, I'll shoot you in the face."

"Stephanie. Don't threaten my mother."

"I'm not worried, Son. When her cousin finds her, he'll give her what she deserves."

SLAM! That bitch shut the door so hard I saw her windows shake.

"FUCKKKKKKK YOUUUUUU!" The bitch peeked through the blinds with her scary ass.

"Let's go, Stephanie. What you doing?" Gary must've heard me and jumped out the car. He lifted me in his arms and told me to shut the fuck up.

"That bitch was—"

"We have to keep a low profile and you're out here yelling." He put me down, grabbed the bag and tossed it on the backseat.

Gary made me sit on the passenger side claiming I was too hostile at the moment and needed to relax.

Pulling off the street I noticed a car following us, well I thought it was until it turned off. My paranoia was getting worse. Maybe it's time to leave this area and devise a plan up for King later.

"That was good." Gary rolled off me breathing heavy. After we returned from Liam's house, we were both aggravated and took our aggression out in the bedroom.

"I'm going to grab the bag out the car." Getting off the bed, I wrapped the robe around my body.

"Where did you put the keys?" He pointed to the chair.

Once I saw him pick the remote for the game up, I knew we mostly likely wouldn't speak for the remainder of the day. He was like a child with that damn thing. It was fine because I planned on leaving him anyway.

Instead of going to the car, I hopped in the shower, got dressed and grabbed my purse and phone. Anything else I'd need could be purchased wherever I'm going. Opening the motel room door, two people walking by scared the hell out of me. They apologized and went about their way.

Approaching the car, a stench overtook my nose. Covering it with my shirt, I opened the back door to get the bag and almost vomited. The smell came from the car but from where. I looked under it as well as all around. Not being able to find it, I went inside the room and saw Gary still playing the game. Thankfully, he wasn't yelling.

"What the hell?" The smell became stronger and this time everything I ate, was released on the floor when I opened the bag. Gary turned around with straight fear on his face after seeing my mother's head inside. Who put it there and where was my money?

"That nigga knows where we are." Soon as he hopped up, his body fell to the floor. A bullet straight between the eyes. I turned to see a guy standing at the doorway with his gun pointed at me.

"You didn't think I'd let you get away that easy, did you?" The guy moved and King stepped in. My body began to shake.

"Take her."

Chapter Twelve

KING

Stephanie thought she was slick staying inside a motel thinking it would throw me off her trail. Little did she know, I've been watching her for a while now but waiting. Because I knew her whereabouts, she wasn't a threat to me or Ivy. Other things had to be taken care of first that were more important.

For instance, Ivy didn't know yet, but I purchased a house for us. It was only a year old but very spacious. There were six bedrooms, seven bathrooms; including in the master suite. That alone had four walk-in closets, two on each side. There was a room connected by the bathroom which I had decorated into a baby's room with all neutral colors. I'm sure Ivy will want our first child as close as possible.

There was a living and dining room but the family room

was even bigger. It also had a bathroom inside and a set of private steps that no one could see. Those stairs made it easier to get into the family room instead of having to walk around the house.

The kitchen was just as big and per Maria, Ivy would love it. Yup, I had her help me decorate that and the guest rooms. I left the master for Ivy to do. I thought about allowing her to do the baby's room but decided against it. She would need as much rest as she could get.

I also planned on having the doctor and nurse, who are husband and wife that they're used t growing up, come over weekly to monitor her. They knew her well and it was my goal to make sure Ivy had a safe and healthy pregnancy.

Shit, I even went and had a conversation with her father. It didn't go the way I thought but knowing the type of man they said he was, I'd say it was fine.

"Why the fuck you here?" Maria had called Noah Sr. down.

"We need to have a conversation."

"We don't need to have shit. You got my daughter involved with that wacko you used to date. Then your family made her miscarry; granted so did the other nigga by cheating but from what I see, you're no better than him." He looked me up and down as Maria shook her head.

"You're wealthy but not as wealthy as me. What can you offer my daughter that her father can't?" I stood in a stance and gave him eye contact. Fathers always respected men who gave them their full attention.

"First of all, she has all my love." He laughed and I felt slightly offended.

"Anyone can say they love someone. Shoot, I love Maria and Mr. Bean but I ain't fucking them. Give me something else." He made follow him into the living room.

"She'll have stability, love, and honorable man, a good father to her children and the perfect husband." Maria had a smile on her face.

"Awww that's cute. My daughter needs more than that."

"How do you know what she needs when you barely show her any love?" He was started to aggravate me and I did try to keep my composure for the most part.

"Watch it, Nigga." I sat down opposite of him.

"My wife was the epitome of perfect in my eyes." I felt a story coming on.

"I never cheated on her, we never had arguments in front of the kids, we gave them whatever they heart desired, and above all, my wife showed them unconditional love even when I didn't."

"Ok."

"I'll admit I'm not a man to express his feelings in public but I do love my children." I can't say he didn't because when they're in trouble he may talk shit but he was always there.

"My daughter witnessed me being mean and awful lot. Not to her mom but to her and her siblings. It had nothing to do with them but more so with the fact, my son had been in a terrible accident and became an addict. Let alone the fact, their mom, my wife was dying. It was a lot for me to handle along with running all the businesses and traveling." He stared off into space for a moment.

"All my wife wanted was for me to make sure the kids were ok when she passed and I couldn't do it. I was so mad at the world, at God for taking her, I lashed out at them." I could see the hurt on his face.

"My son wanted to get clean and didn't do it in enough time to show his mom. When she died, his addiction became even worse. You know I tried to take my own life a few times. It's why those nurse bitches were here in the first place." He laughed.

"They tried to sue and then my son, Noah found out I was showing my dick at work to those bitches and even fucked a few."

"Noah Sr." Maria shouted.

"I have each of those women on tape doing things on their own free will with me. When I told them they were only to satisfy my needs, they claimed sexual abuse. Oh and once one told the others did too, thinking they were gonna get paid." He was aggravated saying that part of the story.

"My lawyer didn't want to use the tapes on court because of who I am. The women could all say they didn't know about the recording and that's another issue. To make it all go away they were paid a small sum of money. Noah Jr. found out and assumed I was a damn pervert so I went with it. I'm an old man that women still want to sleep with. Why would I turn them down when my dick still gets hard?" He shrugged and Maria sucked her teeth.

"I watched all my kids go through things and couldn't do

anything because I had no clue what to do. So, if something came up, money was thrown at them to make it go away."

"Damn."

"I'm telling you this because Ivy Davis, my sweet and naive, Ivy." He was smiling.

"She needs a man to be there for her mentally and emotionally." I understood because she was for sure showing signs of crazy at times.

"If you can give her the stability, honesty and love that she needs then I'm all for you two being together."

"If you can't, then let her go."

"That's never happening and I will do any and everything possible to keep her happy." Believe it or not, I ended up staying over there for hours talking to him. Maria made us dinner and brought out the photo albums.

Ivy was a spitting image of her mother and I was now able to see why he didn't want to let her go. However, he had no choice because that woman was the love of my life.

"You good, bro?" Amerius pulled me out my thoughts when we got to my Aunt Gloria's house. I'm glad he drove because that zone I was in would've made us crash.

"I'm good." Opening the door, I stretched when I got out. It was time to get this over with. I was missing the fuck outta Ivy.

"We're ready." Iesha was dressed in all black. My cousin was down for whatever and didn't give a fuck if a family member had to go. Hence the reason she was there when our aunt took her last breath.

Taking a walk through the house, the photos of me and Amerius growing up were removed. I had some placed in the new house and Amerius did the same at his. There was no need for memories like that to be destroyed.

"What's going on?" Stephanie was standing outside strapped to a tree with her arms and legs out. It reminded me of people who go in those indoor skydiving rides. I walked over to her.

"We're here because this was the exact place you caused my girl to lose our first child." She rolled her eyes.

"How did you get my mother's head?" I moved close so she could hear me.

"Your mother was alive after you shot her." Stephanie had a surprised look on her face.

"She told me everything as far as why you hated my woman, how you set up the kidnappings; pretty much everything."

"That bitch."

"Not very nice to call her that, especially when she went along with your dumb ass schemes." Iesha chimed in.

"When her body went to the morgue after taking her life in the hospital, I paid good money to have her removed. My boy cut her head off and froze it just for me to give it to Liam."

"What?"

"You were so busy talking shit to his mom; you never checked the bag. If you had, you would've known you had her head the entire time." I laughed.

"Liam was in on it and—"

"Liam suffered consequences too once you left his house." Amerius killed him and his mother.

She may not have known about Liam's leisure activities which was basically trying to stalk Ivy, but she knew he had no business dealing with someone like Stephanie and if not, oh well.

"You know, Ivy was never a fighter and the pain you inflicted on her was very harmful her body. So, our beautiful cousin here." I pointed to Iesha.

"Hey, Cuz. It's been a long time." Iesha waved and put on a pair of brass knuckles.

"Just kill me." Stephanie never liked our cousin because she would always curse her out. She also knew Iesha could fight and there was no winning with her even if she wasn't strapped to a tree.

"That would be too easy. I think it would be more fun to watch what's about to happen." She shook her head no as Iesha hooked off.

"Damnnnnn!" Me, Amerius and a few other guys on our team yelled at the same time. Iesha hit her so hard, teeth flew out.

After a few more times, I handed Iesha a metal bat. If Stephanie were a man, I'd be doing all this myself. One of the guys thought it was best to put duct tape on her mouth for the remainder of this. Stephanie most likely didn't have a voice but you can never be sure.

"Take your best shot." I taped a red dot on Stephanie's stomach. Amerius thought it would be funny to do that and printed a big one out for this reason. When Iesha hit her, Stephanie couldn't buckle if she wanted to because her body was stuck in a straight up position.

"Another one and do it harder." Amerius yelled out. Blood was seeping out of Stephanie's mouth and somehow her ribs broke through her skin.

"Because you're stuck to this tree, I can't have her kick you in the back until your neck snapped so I'm gonna do you one better." Two of the guys removed her from the tree.

"Stephanie was clinging to life at this point but I had to get this done so she could really feel Ivy's pain. Looking over at my cousins' tears as Iesha poured gasoline on her, I smiled.

"Now go meet your mother in hell." I placed the lighter by her pants and watched as she went up in flames. When her body stared to smell, I kicked her over into the pool. It may not be exactly what she did to Ivy, but it was close enough in my eyes.

"I'm glad this shit is over." Amerius said, standing on the side of me. Iesha had one of my boys recording her pretending to fight one of the others with the brass knuckles.

"Me too. Now I can finally rest knowing Ivy won't ever feel pain again. Well, she will tonight because I'm taking all my frustration out on her."

"Bye, Nigga. Don't nobody wanna hear that." Amerius walked off.

After my people came to clean up, the house was set ablaze. No one needed to purchase a place like that anyway. I headed straight to Ivy's father house, called her out and drove straight to my house to relieve some stress. I'll take her to our new place tomorrow.

Epilogue

Knox finally got his day in court and the judge threw the case out. His lawyer showed photos of Yasmina out with Knox at the bar. The judge wanted to know how she was suing him but sleeping around at the same time. Also, the lawyer showed the affidavits of Yasmina soliciting Mr. Davis only proving she was basically trying to extort money from the family anyway she could. In the long run, she received no money and broke up with her man after learning about him and her friend creeping. Knox and Mya finally got it together and he was ready to propose in a few months.

Noah completed the program at the rehabilitation center and not only did Kandy show up to get him, so did his entire family and her mom and daughter. When her mom met Noah Sr.

those two argued like crazy but then Maria called Ivy to say Kandy's mom had been visiting a lot.

Ivy was ecstatic when she saw the new house King purchased for them and cried as she walked through it. Ivy threw a house-warming party where King proposed and married her the same day. He paid the mayor a lot of money to come on his day off but it was worth it to King. He wanted his child to have the same last name at birth. He did tell Ivy she could have a bigger one later but she was happy with how it was done the first time.

Everyone lived Happily Ever After!

The End

Coming Soon

Tempting A Billionaire

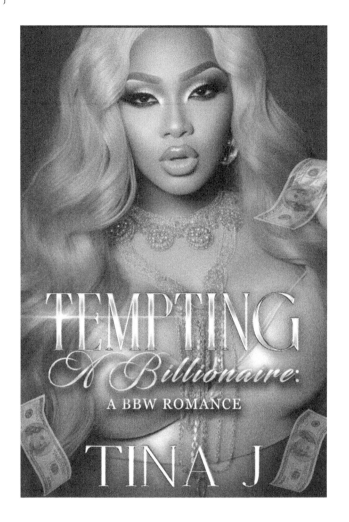

The Don She Fell In Love With

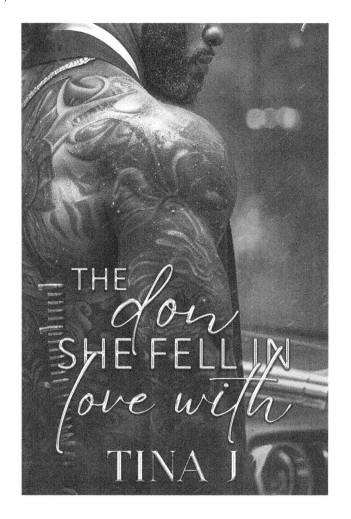

Now Available on Amazon

Bossed Up With A Billionaire

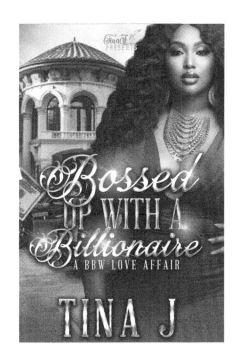

Every Block Boy
Needs A Little Love

Made in United States
Orlando, FL
25 August 2024

50737068R00075